COLD Cash

The Perfect Heist

by Jerry Harju

Jerry Harju

COLD Cash

The Perfect Heist

by Jerry Harju

Cover Design by
Rick Humphrey and Harold Himes

Copyright 1999
Jerry Harju

Published by North Harbor Publishing
Marquette, Michigan 49855

Publishing Coordination by
Globe Printing, Inc.
Ishpeming, Michigan

Printed by
Book Crafters
Chelsea, Michigan

ISBN 0-9670205-0-6
Library of Congress Card No. 99-60788

June 1999

Introduction

Have you ever wondered what it would be like to be an average law-abiding citizen, so far in debt that you'd consider pulling a bank robbery? That's the dilemma of two Upper Michigan heros in "Cold Cash." But not to worry, they've planned the perfect heist. Well . . . maybe not exactly perfect. There are a few complications, not the least of which are a couple of women.

Let me be perfectly clear; this book is a work of fiction and not about my life as my four previous books have been. I have never, repeat *never,* contemplated pulling a bank job as the hero of this book wound up doing.

"Cold Cash" is a fast-moving adventure tale, and I think you'll enjoy reading it. I always like to hear from my readers. Drop me a line and say hello and give me your opinion of the book—no matter what it is.

Jerry Harju
528 E. Arch St. # 1
Marquette, MI 49855
e-mail jharju@bresnanlink.net

Dedication

To Jeff Jacobs, my lifelong friend
and the mastermind of this caper.

Acknowledgements

There are always many people whose expert and able assistance make my books possible.

My deep appreciation to my two editors: Pat Green, my longtime sweetheart, and Karen Murr, my cousin. They now have several books under their belts, and with "Cold Cash" have once again proven that their knowledge of the English language is superior to mine. Rick Humphrey has again produced a charming cover drawing, and Harold Himes skillfully provided the final coloration and cover design. I'm indebted to Myron Hillock, my snowmobile expert, who painlessly introduced me to the fine art of sledding. I thank Circuit Judge Edward Quinnel and researcher Meg Goodrich for providing answers to various legal and technical questions that arose. I also appreciate the police-procedure information furnished by troopers at the Negaunee Post of the Michigan State Police. Suzanne Coron gave me the lowdown on bank security operations. Finally, I thank Jeff Jacobs, Dick Beaudry, Rob Trost, Laverne Chappell, Karen Douglas, Colleen Sheldon, Moira Reynolds, and the folks at the Tuesday night writers' club meetings for providing valuable feedback and advice on the manuscript.

Other books by Jerry Harju

Northern Reflections
Northern D'Lights
Northern Passages
The Class of '57

We paused at the frozen shore and listened. The trooper's snowmobile sounded closer.

McGerk's voice snapped in my earphones. "Let's go!"

I steered the X out onto the snow-covered ice of the Dead River Basin, opened the throttle wide, and headed east. The powerful snowmobile threw back a huge rooster tail of loose snow as we sped down the basin.

"That cop—he jus' came out on th'ice," McGerk said, looking back. "He's 'bout three, four hundred yards behind us. Let's get a move on."

We were already doing sixty-five, plenty fast enough on loose snow, but I gunned the throttle harder.

The X's engine howled, and the machine rose up and flew. The incredibly stiff wind forced me to take a near-horizontal position, causing my helmet to rap against the handlebars every time the big sled bounced off the snow. A black speck on the horizon in front of us exploded in size—an ice-fishing shack. As we shot past, I caught a snapshot glimpse of a lone fisherman gaping at us, open-mouthed.

I pressed the throttle to the limit. The wind and engine noise merged into one steady deafening roar. One single thought kept racing through my head. Two months ago I'd been leading a very normal, legal, actually boring life. How in hell could I have gotten into such a mess in so short a time?

1

"Willya lookit this," Kippy McGerk's thickly accented voice echoed from the grease pit beneath my Oldsmobile. "Yer car's cleaner'n a whistle. Don't see many old ones like that around here."

I impatiently circled the grease pit, stepping gingerly over an oily crankshaft just lying there. "How can it be clean under there? I just drove it over two thousand miles from Los Angeles." I couldn't believe it—I'd been cooling my heels here for a half-hour already and this grease monkey was wasting more of my time admiring the underside of my car.

"I don' mean dirt," McGerk said. "Rust . . . yer car ain't got no rust."

"Rust? Why in hell would it have rust?"

McGerk pulled the oil-pan plug and began draining the motor oil into a large, dented pan. "I guess it wouldn't, bein' a California car. Up here, the road salt eats yer car up—fulla holes in a coupl'a years."

"Road salt?"

McGerk gave me a sideways look. "Don'cha know what road salt is? County spreads it on th'roads all winter t'melt the ice an' snow. Whaddaya doin' up here anyway—you a travelin' salesman or sumthin'?"

I was definitely an "or sumthin'," an out-of-work software engineer taking up writing as a second career.

"I just moved up here," I told McGerk. "Got in this morning." I danced a little jig to keep warm, watching my breath form wispy little clouds. Sure as hell I was going to catch pneumonia standing around in this rundown garage. If it gets this cold in November, what's January going to be like?

McGerk looked up at me with amazement. "Ya *moved* up *here*? From *California*? In *November*? What's yer name anyway?" He wanted to get all the facts straight before spreading the story around town about this crazy Californian who moved here just before winter set in and didn't even know what road salt was.

"Joe Jarvi," I answered.

McGerk shook his head, puzzled. "Everybody in Upper Michigan wants t'move *outta* here. Get someplace warm, away from th'winters. People mus' think yer crazy."

Well, that was true. At my going-away party in Santa Monica, friends and former Digitek associates had bombarded me with good-natured jabs regarding the sanity of swapping the land of perpetual sunshine for the brutal Siberia-like climate of Upper Michigan.

"Of all th'places ya could'a moved, whyd'ya pick here?" McGerk asked.

"I just wrapped up a computer job in California and decided I needed a change of scenery," I said offhandedly. Not exactly true, of course.

An icy gust of wind speared through the open garage door, slashing through my fashionable California windbreaker like it was a net undershirt.

"Is there any reason why you can't shut that door?" I asked.

McGerk climbed out of the pit, closed the big wooden sliding door, and turned on the overhead fluorescent light. "Keep it open during th'day. Saves on the light bill."

McGerk was about my age, not bad looking with blonde hair, bright blue eyes, and a lazy, boyish grin. A barber and some clean clothes would have worked wonders. As it was, his long shaggy hair, two-weeks' growth of beard, and greasy coveralls fit in perfectly with the sloppy garage and its dirty rags, piles of empty motor-oil containers, and engine parts strewn all over.

He popped the Olds's hood latch and opened several quarts of oil. "So yer a computer geek, huh? People been tellin' me I ought'a get one a them PC's."

"I'm not in the computer business anymore. I'm a writer." Not true either. Not yet at least.

"Oh? Whaddaya write about?"

I avoided the question. "How much longer is this gonna take?"

"Not long. Gotta replace yer windshield-washer fluid with antifreeze. Wanna put on some winter blades?"

"Winter blades?" I didn't know what was going on here. I only knew that my Uncle Paul warned me that the temperature was going down to zero tonight, and I'd better get my California car down here right away to be winterized. I didn't even know what the hell winterizing was.

McGerk opened a drawer beneath the cluttered workbench and held up a huge, rubber-covered windshield-wiper blade. "Better'n what ya got there—helps take off the ice an' snow in the mornings."

"C'mon, those blades on my car are almost brand-new."

"Gotta garage t'keep th'car in?"

"I don't even have an apartment yet. I'm staying with my aunt and uncle till I find a place." I slapped my hands against my thighs to keep the blood moving.

"Apartments in Ishpeming don' usually have garages. Bein' outside, th'car'll get pretty icy. Buy th'blades—don' cost much. Ought'a get some all-weather tires, too."

"Those tires don't even have ten thousand miles on them."

"Yeah, but that kind'a tread ain't worth a damn on the snow. Another thing—get a new battery. If th'car's outside when the weather gets below freezin', yer gonna have trouble crankin' her up with th'one ya got."

"Save the sales pitch. I'm a little short of cash right now." I'd heard a lot of the you-need-this-you-need-that crap from money-grubbing mechanics I'd dealt with over the years in California.

McGerk shrugged and proceeded to leave a perfect set of ten grimy fingerprints on the front edge of the Olds's hood as he slammed it down. "Suit yerself. I don' sell tires or batteries anyhow."

After McGerk had finished with the car, I drove back to my uncle's house.

I'd been in Ishpeming only one other time, with my parents when I was a kid. It was early October, and every street was lined with trees all decked out in brilliantly colored leaves, like paintings I'd seen. I'd loved it.

But now, in November, the town in no way resembled the autumn wonderland of yellows, reds, and oranges that I remembered. The leaves were dark, soggy corpses littering the ground, and the trees raised their bare limbs to the sky in surrender to the onset of winter. Maybe this guy McGerk was right. Maybe moving here *was* crazy.

But I'd had to move *somewhere*. I couldn't afford to live in Southern California any longer. After the layoff, my ex-employer, Digitek—one of those software firms run by twenty-something computer nerds—tried to help me find another job, assigning a human-resources weenie to cook up a highly exaggerated resume. But the job market was tight. All of the computer companies in the area were trimming their own fat, and the resume only generated polite rejection letters.

Without a steady income—the puny unemployment check notwithstanding—the payments on the ocean-view apartment and prized BMW with the white-leather interior began gobbling up my meager savings like a school of piranha. Things got tight in a hurry. In desperation, I'd casually suggested to my flight-attendant girlfriend that it would be cozy and ever-so-romantic if I moved in with her. She didn't agree. Her lifestyle didn't allow for taking in unemployed boyfriends. If fact, she'd recommended quite the opposite--go our separate ways to see if we missed each other. As it turned out, we didn't.

I'd approached my parents, though not a viable option since they'd just made a down payment on a new condo in a Laguna Miguel retirement village. My father sighed when I mentioned a loan, and not just because they couldn't afford to bail me out. For years he'd harangued me about my lifestyle. Why did I have to live in Marina del Rey, the most expensive area on the west side? What was wrong with Culver City? I owned *fourteen* suits? Who needs fourteen suits? The ongoing argument reached its zenith when, in a moment of absolute stupidity, I mentioned the price tag on my new BMW. He went through the roof.

My mother knew that the loan wasn't going to happen and began talking about Upper Michigan. The cost of living was much lower than California. Besides, her sister Edna in Ishpeming would be more than happy to put me up until I got my feet on the ground. And maybe I should just take some time off and write that book I'd been talking about for years.

I remembered the fall colors and it sounded like a good idea. Besides, Upper Michigan—about as far north as you can get in the lower forty-eight—was the logical location to write my novel. Okay, so I'm a romantic. Maybe I wasn't cut out to be a computer genius in the first place.

I bounced the BMW back to the dealer—my equity barely covering the balance of payments—sold off everything else, bought a relatively clean but well-used Oldsmobile, packed it full of clothing and personal gear, and took off for Michigan to begin a new life at age thirty-two.

Paul and Edna Jarvi still lived in the same narrow, two-story wood-frame house I'd visited so many years ago. It seemed smaller now, although the wide front porch still looked comfortable. This just wasn't the season to be sitting on it.

We sat down at the old dining-room table promptly at five-thirty—dinnertime in any respectable Finnish household. Aunt Edna, an affable, roly-poly woman, took great pride in her softball-size meatballs, generously heaping three onto my plate with assurances that there were plenty more where that came from. I gratefully dug in. I'd been one of those Southern California health fanatics, eating nothing but fish, chicken, fresh fruits, vegetables, and whole-grain bread, but McGerk's icy garage had changed that.

Paul Jarvi, a hulking mountain of a man, sat across the table from me, staring with flinty, suspicious eyes at the meatballs on my plate. When I'd arrived in town early that morning I'd told him about moving up here permanently and asked if I could stay with them until I found a place. Paul had nodded grudgingly, but I could see the wheels turning. His salary at the flooring mill obviously left no margin for extras, and clearly he wasn't about to provide long-term room and board for freeloading relatives.

"I see there's plenty of apartments listed in the *Mining Journal*," Paul said.

Edna shot him a severe look. "Paul, he just got into town. Give the boy a chance to catch his breath."

"The good ones get snapped up pretty quick," he continued.

"I'll start looking around tomorrow," I said, alternating my attention between Paul and the huge meatball I was carving up.

"The Sunday *Journal*'s also got jobs listed," Paul added. "That dry cleaner over on Division Street is lookin' for a steam presser. No experience necessary—they'll train ya."

Edna looked disgusted. "Joe's got a college degree in computers, Paul. He can find a better-paying job than dry cleaning."

"The Post Office is lookin' fer people, too. Gotta take an exam though--probably have to study up fer it."

"Paul—stop it!"

"I'm going to write a book," I said, picking up a piece of meatball with my fork.

Edna was immediately interested. "Oh, really! What kind of book?"

I hesitated, but thought, what the hell. "It's going to be a north-country novel, sort of a romance."

Paul snorted sarcastically. "Romance? Hah! Seems t'me that with a college degree ya ought'a be able t'do sumthin' more useful'n writin' books 'bout love. A college graduate should be able t'design a sawmill or sumthin' like that."

"I'll pick up some kind of software job until my writing starts to produce income."

"Software jobs—don't think there's too much of that around here," Paul said. "Hope ya got enough money to live on till ya get a paycheck."

"Paul! Quit prying into Joe's affairs."

"Gonna have expenses," Paul added. "Gotta pay a month's rent in advance, gas for the car, car insurance, lot'sa things."

"Don't worry," I replied. "I've got enough money to last for awhile." Again, not true.

"Yer gonna need winter clothes right away—lookit them skimpy things he's wearin', Edna. What size shoe d'ya wear?"

"Nine."

"Smaller than me—I take a twelve. My old rubber boots--swampers we call 'em—will be a li'l on the big side, but they'll do until ya get sum new ones. In th'winter ya wanna wear 'em with lots of socks anyhow."

"And you can give him that old mackinaw jacket in the upstairs closet," Edna volunteered.

After dinner Paul climbed up the narrow, wooden stairwell and returned with the boots and mackinaw. I put them on.

The image in the dining-room mirror looked like a Peanuts cartoon character dressed up to play in the snow. My fingertips barely peeked out from the mackinaw sleeves, and my feet swam around in the big, ugly boots. But in my present financial condition, I couldn't be picky.

Edna looked me over, searching hard for something flattering to say. "Well, at least you'll be warm."

2

*A*t the curb outside my apartment, McGerk's rusted-out old pickup truck and my Olds faced each other with hoods open, looking as though they were chatting about the winter weather. The second snowfall of the week had deposited another two inches on the ground overnight.

McGerk clipped his set of jumper cables to my car battery. "Dollarwise, it don' make any sense. This's the sixth time I jump-started yer car in three weeks. At seven dollars a pop, that's forty-two bucks. Ya could'a had a brand-new, heavy-duty battery half paid for by now. At least, don'cha know anybody who'll come over an' jump-start ya for free?"

I glumly watched my breath drift off into the gray early-morning sky while thumping the long mackinaw sleeves on my thighs to stir up the blood in my arms and hands.

"My uncle did it a couple of times. But then, like you, he started harping at me about getting a new battery. I don't know anybody else well enough to ask. I can't afford a battery, or anything else for that matter. I'm just squeaking by from one payday to the next. By the time I buy food and gas and pay the rent, the money's gone."

The small, furnished second-floor studio apartment I was renting on Ironwood Street was a far cry from my former luxury apartment overlooking the Pacific Ocean. The only view from the small window in my present place was the dilapidated house next door. The furniture consisted of a sagging sofabed, a small two-burner gas range, one cigarette-scarred wooden table, three mismatched chairs, and a thirty-year-old refrigerator. Even at that, the rent barely fit into my budget.

"I know th'pay at the flooring mill ain't that great," McGerk said, "but I thought everybody had t'pay computer geeks lot'sa money."

"Maybe in California, but not up here. Hell, I was lucky to find a job even *using* a computer. Paul had to pull some strings at the mill to even get me a job as a data entry clerk. The pay is terrible but it's all I could find."

McGerk started up his old truck. "Didn't I hear ya mention sumthin' about writin'?"

I got behind the wheel of the Olds. "I'm just getting started at it, and it's not going very well."

Every night I was forcing myself to sit down and laboriously crank out a page or two on the novel, but after eight hours of pounding numbers into an obsolete PC at the flooring mill, followed by a TV dinner in my dumpy little apartment with its clanking steam radiator, I wasn't inspired to write about romance. To make matters worse, I'd sold my PC in California because it was too bulky to transport in the car, and all I had was an old typewriter that Edna had loaned to me. When the correction fluid got too thick, the whole page had to be typed over. It was brutal work.

McGerk gave me the now-familiar hand signal to turn over the Olds's engine. The old car coughed and grudgingly stuttered to life. He coiled up his jumper cables and slammed down the hoods of both vehicles.

I counted the dollar bills in my wallet. "Can I pay you on Friday? I'm a little short right now."

McGerk waved the whole thing off. "Forget it—save yer money fer writin' lessons. You kin buy me a beer some night."

Over the next few days I kept recalling McGerk's comment about writing lessons. On Saturday I drove over to the Northern Michigan University campus in Marquette, the county seat fourteen miles away. On the University Center bulletin board, one particular notice caught my eye. I jotted down the phone number and called that evening.

A woman answered the phone.

"Is Mr. Chris Arquette there?" I asked.

"There *is* no *Mr.* Chris Arquette. I'm Christine Arquette."

The following night I pulled up at a stylish, old Victorian house on Arch Street in Marquette. A woman my age opened the massive front door.

"Christine Arquette?" I asked.

"You must be my new writing student. Come in, but call me Chris." She glanced with curiosity at my oversized mackinaw jacket and the mammoth swampers.

Chris looked at me with large brown eyes that seemed to smile. Her glasses--not fancy ones--enhanced her pretty face. No makeup, but she looked good without it. Her long blonde hair was pulled back in a ponytail and fastened with a leather thong. Even that looked good.

She led me into a large, high-ceiling living room with tall bookshelves lining three walls. A beautiful antique oak writing desk sat next to the tall casement windows. Beethoven's Sixth Symphony flowed softly from hidden speakers. An ideal writer's refuge. I wondered when I'd be able to afford something like this.

"You're young," she said. "Most people who want writing lessons are older, usually retired."

I handed her my thin manuscript. "You wanted to see something I've written. It's going to be a novel, but I haven't gotten very far on it yet."

For the next half-hour we sat side by side as Chris read and reread the manuscript. I nodded in agreement each time she made a comment or suggestion but really wasn't paying much attention to what she was saying. I was too distracted by the woman herself—she was captivating.

She had stopped talking and was waiting for an answer.

"What did you say?" I blurted out.

She smiled, knowing where my mind was. "I said, this is typewritten. Why aren't you using a computer?"

"I sold my old PC when I left L.A. I plan to buy a new Pentium once I get settled." I didn't mention that my current financial situation wasn't going to allow for *any* kind of PC, no matter *how* settled I got.

"Good. Get one soon," she said. "Strong, clean writing requires a lot of editing, and a word processor enables you to do it quickly."

She continued. "You've got some good thoughts here, Joe. Your work has promise. However, I can think of several changes that will enable you to focus your ideas and character development more effectively. If you like, we could have weekly lessons on some of the basics of writing mechanics."

"That would be fine," I said, concealing my delight by nervously mangling the manuscript with both hands. I knew she was doing it for money, but it was incredible that this fascinating woman was going to work with me every week. I didn't even ask what it would cost. It didn't matter—I'd cut back on food.

Chris saw me to the door. "California, huh? What made you move up here?"

"I thought it was a good idea to research the locale of the story." Telling her the truth was the furthest thing from my mind.

She smiled with those eyes again. "I also see that the story's going to have a strong love interest. Are you researching that, too?"

Before I could answer, she quickly apologized, her face coloring slightly. "I'm sorry, I hardly know you and have no business prying into your personal life." Then, she added playfully, "But of course, good writers always thoroughly research their subjects."

The Wild Goose Bar in Ishpeming had been in business since long before prohibition, and the beat-up furnishings and equipment seemed to date back that far. Several hand-lettered signs tacked to the grimy wall behind the bar advertised bargain liquor prices and warned patrons against rowdy behavior and smuggling in their own liquor. An ancient jukebox blared a soulful country-western ballad.

It was Monday, the night after my writing session with Chris, and I was buying McGerk the beer I owed him for jump-starting my car several days before.

I thought it strange—considering our first encounter—that I was gravitating toward a friendship with McGerk. His fractured English advertised the fact that he had very little formal education, but he certainly wasn't stupid. Though cheerful and outgoing, McGerk seemed to be a lone wolf, not wanting or needing friends of either sex. Yet for some reason he liked me, and *I* certainly needed a friend.

"Writin' lessons?" McGerk exclaimed. "I wuz just kiddin' when I said that. How kin ya afford writin' lessons if ya can't even buy a damned battery?"

"I don't know how I'll do it, but I *have* to take those lessons, no matter how broke I am. That woman—I can't get her out of my mind. She's good-looking and smart. She had some great suggestions about my manuscript last night. My work shows promise, she said. I really think she likes me."

"So, go for it."

"There's a problem. I need a PC. Do you know what a good new one costs?—about two thousand dollars. How am I going to manage that?"

McGerk grabbed a handful of popcorn from a bowl on the bar and jammed it into his mouth. "Tell her th'truth. Yer broke an' can't afford it."

"I can't do *that*. She's an assistant professor in the English Department at the university. Lives in a classy Victorian house in east Marquette. Think I'd stand a chance with her if she finds out I'm practically on welfare?"

I pointed to the size-twelve swampers on my feet. "And these damned things! I must have looked like some dumb yokel fresh out of the sticks, clumping into her house last night in my secondhand clothes. I need new winter clothes, but I can't afford *them* either."

"Don'cha have a credit card?" McGerk asked.

"She doesn't wear a wedding or engagement ring," I muttered to no one in particular. "She must be around thirty or so. Probably divorced or widowed."

"Credit card?" McGerk repeated.

"I heard you. I had three credit cards in California but destroyed them after I lost my job at Digitek—too much of a temptation." During the most recent jump-start, I'd confided in McGerk about the layoff and my financial woes.

"Besides, I can't afford to run up anything on credit right now."

McGerk looked at me in amazement. "Whaddaya talking about? *Nobody* pays off a credit card. Ya pay th'minimum amount every month—about two, three percent of what ya owe. It's nuthin—less than a phone bill fer crissake."

He sipped his beer and chuckled. "Here ya find a great-lookin', smart woman who kin help ya with yer writin', and yer scared of runnin' up a coupl'a bills. Ya gotta take a few chances in life if yer ever gonna get anywhere. Who knows? A year or two from now ya might have yer new book in every bookstore in th'country and that professor chick'll be beggin' you t'speak to her university class 'bout how t'be a successful writer."

I took a deep gulp of beer, half-listening to a country-western song lamenting unrequited love. "You're right. I'll go down to one of the banks tomorrow."

Computer Cache, a new store in the Westwood Mall in Marquette, specialized in personal computers, accessories, and software. A salesclerk, ten years my junior, intercepted me at the door.

"May I help you?"

"I'm in the market for a PC," I said.

"You're in luck. We just received a shipment of the new Pentium 5000."

"I don't need anything too fancy. I'm a writer and just want something with a good word processor."

He smiled at that remark. "A year from now, the Pentium 5000 will be the new standard, and all the latest software will require it. Wouldn't be wise to settle for anything less."

With that, the clerk expertly steered me over to a PC that was amusing itself by playing a sub-par round of golf at Augusta National.

He waved at the computer, using his pen as a wand. "This configuration has the 32-megabyte synchronous DRAM, 512K pipelined burst cache, five megabytes of 3-D 64-Bit PCI graphics, a 48X CD-ROM drive, 3.5 inch diskette drive, *and* 9.2 gigabytes of EIDE hard drive."

He quickly bent over the curved, ergonomically correct keyboard. "A writer, huh? Look at *this* word processor." He punched a few keys, and the computer instantly forgot about golf and flashed a series of software titles. The screen turned blue and the cursor blinked impatiently, waiting for the user to begin typing.

"This is the new Word Wizard—standard software with the Pentium 5000. Aside from the regular dictionary, it has a six-hundred-thousand-word thesaurus. Give me a word."

"Love."

He typed in "love," hit a function key, and the Pentium 5000 immediately pounced on it, producing a long string of synonyms—affection, ardor, attachment, devotion, fondness, sentiment, passion, sex . . .

"I'll take it," I said.

"Very good. Now, the monitor is extra, of course. I'd recommend the new Viviscan 24-inch with 1600 by 1200 ultra-high non-interlaced resolution and 96Hz refresh rate."

"Sounds good."

"And I imagine you'll be needing a printer?"

"Of course."

The clerk led me over to a large, ivory-colored printer squatting on a long table.

"Since you're a writer, you'll be cranking out manuscripts continually and need speed. This is the latest laser printer—sharp 1200 by 1200 dpi resolution with a thirty-page-per-minute engine. They don't come any faster than that. Shall I include this?"

"Why not?"

We walked over to a desk, and he began jotting down my purchases on an order pad. "Will this be cash or charge?"

I whipped out my brand-new Hematite First National Bank credit card.

❄

Getz's Clothiers in Marquette caters to the most discriminating Upper Michigan man. As I entered, a silver-haired gentleman attired in a pinstriped dress shirt, coordinating tie, and sharply creased trousers cast a critical eye at my swampers and mackinaw. He approached warily. "May I assist you?"

"I need some winter boots—top of the line."

The salesman thawed a bit. "That would be Sorel." He inspected my swampers. "About a size twelve?"

"No, about a size nine."

He produced a pair of fine leather Sorels with thick liners. They were adequate for everyday wear in the snow, but I wanted something with more sex appeal for my writing-lesson evenings. We added a pair of slim black boots.

"Something in a winter jacket?" the salesman asked hopefully, glancing at Paul's mackinaw.

I quickly peeled off the old coat and handed it to him. "Put this and these old boots in a paper sack, and I'll take them when I leave."

During the next two hours I picked out a Nautica winter coat with special hand-warmer pockets, eight dress shirts, three heavy sweaters, six pairs of slacks, and a tweed Hart, Schaffner, and Marx sports coat with leather elbow patches, suitable for attending writers' functions.

The salesman was especially friendly now, convinced that I had to be a backwoods eccentric who had wandered into the big city after making a killing in the fur market. "I'll help you take the parcels to your car as soon as I total up your purchases. "Will this be cash or charge?"

I handed him the Hematite First National credit card.

3

Fat snowflakes spiraled into my headlights as I drove to Marquette for the second writing lesson with Chris. I crept along at a turtle's pace and with good reason. Several times—particularly after a light snow—I'd applied the brakes at a stop sign only to have the car go into an alarming spin. I was praying that I wouldn't total the Olds before I mastered the art of winter driving.

Chris looked me over as I stamped my feet on her doormat. "You have new clothes."

"Oh, uh-huh," I replied, attempting to sound casual. "I finally found the time to shop for my winter wardrobe."

I mentioned my new Pentium 5000 and gave her a revised copy of the manuscript, the product of several days of laborious editing with the Word Wizard processor.

She scanned the pages and nodded approvingly.

We got down to business. Chris discussed the basics of good writing—reducing verbiage, improving story flow, restructuring sentences—while we reviewed my manuscript in detail.

Again I was trying hard to concentrate, but huddling together over the single copy of the manuscript made it impossible. Every so often her arm would brush against me as she made a notation on one of the pages. I could feel her body heat.

At the end of the session I reluctantly put my boots and coat on and headed for the front door. I opened the heavy door but didn't step out.

There was at least eight inches of snow on the ground, and it was still coming down. My car parked at the curb looked like a giant marshmallow.

Chris looked out from behind me. "You can't drive in that. You'll have to stay here tonight—the roads won't be completely plowed till morning."

I wanted to run outside and kiss each snowflake. "I could stay at one of those motels on the highway," I offered halfheartedly.

"Joe, just look at the street. How would you even *get* to a motel? Come back inside, you're letting the cold air in."

She brought out sheets, a pillow, and blankets for the big sofa in the living room. And a pair of men's pajamas. She retired to the back bedroom without volunteering any information about who the pajamas belonged to.

I turned out the living-room lamps and stretched out under the blankets, wide awake, thinking about Chris just a few steps away in the bedroom. Is she expecting me to get up and go into the bedroom? No—she isn't that type. She didn't hesitate to tell me to spend the night, though. But who wouldn't?—it was snowing like hell out there.

Suddenly Chris appeared in the entrance to the living room, her loose hair flowing onto the shoulders of her long white nightgown.

"I've set the alarm for seven o'clock. They plow all night, and the roads should to be open by then. You won't be too late for work." Smiling, she looked at me for a moment and then turned and went back into the bedroom.

Why did she stand there smiling at me? Was it an invitation? No, she was just being friendly. If I go into the bedroom now, I'll screw up any chance I may have in the future. I'll bet she didn't know that the lamp behind her was shining through her nightgown. At least I don't *think* she knew. Maybe I'm blowing the chance of a lifetime.

It took me a long time to get to sleep.

The Wild Goose Bar was holding a pool tournament and the place was crowded. I bought McGerk a Budweiser in payment for another jump-start a few mornings before.

"McGerk, I think I'm falling in love."

"Me too," he replied, ogling a tight-T-shirted redhead leaning over the pool table.

"I'm serious. I stayed over at Chris's house last night."

McGerk tore his eyes away from the girl. "Congratulations. That wuz fast."

"No, no, not that. I slept on the sofa. Couldn't get home because of the snowstorm."

McGerk immediately lost interest in my pseudo-romantic adventure and drained his Bud. "Ya wanna make an advance payment on tomorrow morning's jump-start?"

I held up two fingers to the bartender. "This is tricky with her being my writing teacher. I have to figure out my next move."

"How 'bout asking her out on a dinner date? Ya got new clothes now."

"Yeah. Where's a good place to take her around here?"

"Well, ain't been there myself, but if she's as classy as ya say, an' y'wanna impress her, take 'er to dinner at the Landmark Inn in Marquette. Ritziest place in the county."

"Expensive?"

McGerk laughed. "I heard ya kin get two dinners and sum pretty good wine fer only 'bout a hunnert dollars."

"Jeezuz! A new PC, new clothes, hundred-dollar dinners. This is starting to run into real money."

McGerk drank half of his fresh Bud and let out a tooth-rattling belch. "Chasin' women usually does. Don't forget yer credit card."

The Landmark Inn on Front Street in Marquette features two luxurious dining rooms. The first-floor restaurant, adjacent to the large European-styled lobby, provides sufficiently elegant surroundings for guests who want a fine dinner for a special occasion. But those who seek a truly unique dining experience choose the Sky Room on the top floor.

Chris and I got off the elevator and walked across the plush medallion-design carpet to the Sky Room entrance where the maitre d' promptly escorted us to a window table overlooking the harbor on Lake Superior. A waiter quietly lit the candle, casting a mellow glow on the table's fine silver and crystal.

But Chris's stunning appearance paled the surroundings. She was wearing an ankle-length, very Bohemian, deep azure crepe dress. Subtle eye makeup, a faint blush of lip gloss, and something special with her hair completed the magical effect. As usual, I couldn't take my eyes off of her.

Finally, I picked up the leather-bound wine list and studied it. Having dined in many upscale Los Angeles restaurants during my more affluent days, I was familiar with good wines, but the French varieties on this list were new to me. They were also an order of magnitude more expensive.

"May I suggest the wine?" I asked. "They have a good French

merlot." I'd never heard of the label, but at thirty dollars a bottle it was the least expensive item on the list.

Moments later, a burgundy-jacketed wine steward appeared with the bottle and reverently held it out for my inspection. I scrutinized the label and nodded. He poured an ounce into my crystal wine glass and waited expectantly for the verdict. I sipped and nodded again, and both glasses were filled.

Soon Chris's eyes sparkled from the wine and the excitement of the occasion, and she was eager to talk.

"I don't know very much about you, but when we met, you said you had a job at the flooring mill. You don't look like the type who'd be working at a flooring mill."

While refilling the wine glasses, I quickly organized my thoughts and launched into a newly invented work scenario, choosing my words carefully.

"As you probably know, everything is run by computers nowadays. The mill is in the process of upgrading their production system, and I have a consulting contract to advise them on their software requirements."

Chris was astounded. "The Ishpeming flooring mill has hired a software consultant?"

The wine warmed me to the subject, and I began to wing it even further. "That's right. I have consulting contracts with other companies as well—all over the country. But I deal with them by phone or FAX. The flooring mill is the only contract that currently requires my presence." I was shoveling it on pretty thick, but what the hell.

"I'm impressed that you've become so well connected up here in such a short time. What's your background?"

That one was easy, I could stick pretty much to the truth. I told her about being born and raised in West Los Angeles, the computer science degree from UCLA and my position at Digitek Systems developing on-board software for communications satellites. I omitted the fact that it was a mundane job working on a tiny segment of obscure network protocol software and I had absolutely no idea how it fit into the grand scheme of things. Naturally, I didn't mention the layoff.

"My software career—even in the aerospace industry—got pretty boring after a few years. Not my real calling. Once I become proficient at writing and know that I can write novels that will sell, I'll phase out the consulting work entirely."

Chris laughed and then apologized. "I'm sorry, I don't mean to make light of your career goals, but I always tell my writing students not to give up their day jobs."

"Well, I *do* have a nest egg," I said casually. The French merlot must have been getting to me because the lies were turning into real whoppers.

The waiter appeared and we ordered. I selected the chicken satay appetizer, haricot vert salad, an intermezzo of lemon sorbet, and the entree of medallions of veal presented with cold water lobster. There were no prices on the menu. Apparently, the Landmark Inn assumed that if cost is a factor, you'd come to the wrong place.

Over the salad I said, "I was pleased yet somewhat surprised when you accepted my dinner invitation, inasmuch as I'm one of your writing students."

"I've never done that before. Of course, my other private students are a lot older. Actually, this is my first date since the divorce—too busy with university activities, I guess."

"Divorce?"

"A year ago. After the papers were signed, he took off for parts unknown. He was always scrambling around, coming up with crackpot schemes for getting rich, none of which ever panned out. We had a lot of arguments about money. You're not like him at all. You're stable, know what you want to do with your life, and have sufficient financial security to make it happen."

I took a big gulp of wine.

Chris talked more as we proceeded through dinner. She'd been raised in an academic environment. Her mother and father were both professors at McGill University in Montreal. After graduating from high school with honors, she moved to the United States and earned a B.A. and M.A. in journalism from the University of Michigan. Wanting to teach also, she accepted a position at Northern Michigan University in Marquette and four years later became an assistant professor in the English Department. Her short, rocky marriage was the only blip in an otherwise serene life.

Up to that point, the dinner had been routine, get-acquainted, first-date stuff. Then, something unexpected happened over the Irish coffee. Maybe it was *because* of the Irish coffee, I don't know. The conversation slowed to a halt, and we began trading long sensual glances across the table. Chris extended her hand and I immediately took it.

The silent messages had grown even stronger by the time the waiter arrived to present the check. I didn't even flinch at the amount, although I noted that McGerk's estimate was considerably off target—on the low side. Without taking my eyes off of Chris, I held out my credit card to the waiter.

The snow was falling in thick flakes as we left the Landmark.

Chris smiled teasingly. "I'm feeling a little high. How about you?"

"Maybe a bit," I replied, trying to sound in control as I carefully navigated across the parking lot. I felt like I was on ice skates, except I'd never been on ice skates.

"It's only three blocks to my place. Let's walk." She stuck her tongue out, catching snowflakes on it. She put her face up close to mine, her extended tongue almost touching my lips, then pulled away at the last minute.

"The Landmark won't care if I leave the car here?"

"You can leave the car here all night if you like. They won't mind."

"All night?"

"That's right. If it makes you feel any better, leave a note on the windshield telling them that you're off doing research on your romance novel."

I gripped her hand tightly and we headed off through the snow.

Someone was shaking my shoulder in the darkness. I knew I wasn't in my own bed because the mattress didn't have that familiar spine-crushing sag in the middle.

Then, an ear nibble. "You've got to get up and go home," Chris murmured.

The memory of the previous evening and early morning hours bounded joyfully back into my consciousness. I stretched lazily. "What time is it?"

"Six o'clock."

"But it's Saturday. It *is* Saturday, isn't it?"

"That's right, but you still have to go."

I ran my hand over her warm, rounded stomach. I was feeling magnificent. "What's the hurry? I don't have to go to work today. Besides, it's still dark."

"That's the point. You have to leave before daylight."

I groaned. "Why?"

"This isn't the big city. Everyone on this street knows everyone else. I know it's the nineties, but the head of the English department at the university—my boss—is a real prude, and if the word got around that some guy was seen leaving my house in the morning, it wouldn't do my reputation much good."

She removed my hand and gently nibbled on each finger. "Which brings up my next point. This wasn't a one-night stand, was it?"

"Are you kidding? I want to see you every chance I get."

"Then, we've got to start using your place in Ishpeming. At least I could leave in the morning with some hope of not being recognized."

I bolted upright, instantly awake. "*My* place?"

4

*M*cGerk was slouched on his regular stool at the Wild Goose, his mackinaw draped over the adjacent seat, saving it for me. He'd ordered a Budweiser for each of us.

I handed him his jacket and sat down. "You've got to help me."

"Fer crissake, yer meltin' down that charge card fer every other damned thing. Why don'cha buy yerself a battery already?"

"It's not the battery. I've got to get another apartment."

"Why? Ya jus' got settled in."

I told him about the latest romantic development and my early morning conversation with Chris.

McGerk chuckled knowingly. "Movin's a lotta work. Jus' getta bigger bed."

"C'mon, she thinks I'm a high-priced software consultant. I can't take her to that dump of mine. I need your help. Where can I find a really nice, furnished apartment in Ishpeming?"

. McGerk scratched the stubble on his chin, thinking. "Yesterday, a mine supervisor brought his big Lincoln in fer a lube an' oil. I think he said he was rentin' an apartment up on that hill over in West Ishpeming. Nice area. But the company's sendin' him back to Cleveland an' he's packin' up right now."

"How can I get hold of him? I don't have much time."

"The phone number's on his bill at th'garage."

The following morning McGerk rode over to West Ishpeming with me. Frank Thomas, the landlord, and Ernie Chambers, the mine supervisor and soon-to-be ex-tenant, were both at the apartment to meet us. We shook hands all around.

Chambers invited us in. "Your timing is perfect. I have to be in Cleveland by the end of the week, so I'll be out of here in two or three days."

The sunken living room had deep-pile beige carpeting, a large wood-burning fireplace, and an oversized picture window framing a dark expanse of pine trees. A long sectional sofa and matching recliner faced a teak entertainment center housing a big-screen TV.

Three steps above the living room, separated by a wrought-iron railing, was the dining area furnished with a Danish-modern table and chairs. The kitchen was entirely built in—range, refrigerator, microwave, and dishwasher. The bedroom had a big walk-in closet, dresser, another TV set, and *a king-size bed.*

It was perfect.

"I'll take it," I said.

Thomas seemed surprised that I didn't even ask how much the rent was. "I'll get it cleaned up this weekend," he said.

"Can you clean it before then? I have to be moved in by Friday night—Christmas Eve. I'll be entertaining."

McGerk smothered a laugh.

Thomas nodded in agreement. "Will you need any help moving your furniture in?"

"Isn't this apartment furnished?"

"Oh, no—all of the furniture belongs to him," Thomas explained, nodding at Chambers.

"I'll buy the furniture," I stated flatly to Chambers. "All of it. Name your price."

After the deal was done, McGerk and I headed back to town.

"I know I tol' ya to take a few chances and not be afraid to run up some bills, but ain'tcha gettin' a li'l carried away? How ya gonna pay th'rent on that place? Landlords don't take credit cards, y'know. An' ya tol' Chambers you'd give him a check for th'furniture in two days. Where's *that* money comin' from?"

I produced an envelope, removed a check, and handed it to McGerk.

He held it up to the light from the car window. "Five thousand dollars! Made out to you? What's this for?"

I pointed at the top of the check. "See which bank the check is drawn on? Hematite First National, right here in Ishpeming. They also enclosed a friendly letter urging me to cash it. I've been running up so many charges on their credit card that the bank figures I'm a top-qualified consumer, and they've extended my credit limit. I'll cash the check, and they'll add that amount to what I owe them. The five thousand'll nicely cover the rent and what Ernie Chambers wants for his furniture, with a few bucks left over."

"How much ya owe on that credit card now?"

"I don't know, haven't gotten a statement yet. Besides, like you said, just make the minimum monthly payment."

A stop sign loomed up ahead. I applied the brakes, and the car skidded dangerously on the hard-packed snow, finally sliding to a stop crosswise in the intersection.

By now I was getting to be an old hand at skids. It didn't bother me a bit anymore. But McGerk had been whiteknuckling the dashboard, bracing for a crash.

"While yer dabblin' in all this high finance, think about some snow tires, will ya?"

Moving into the new apartment was a simple operation. I only had to carry over my clothes and the PC equipment. Ernie Chambers—besides selling me the furniture—had included everything in the kitchen cabinets, the bed linens, and even the pictures on the walls. By Thursday evening I was all settled in.

I did have to buy an answering machine. There wasn't a phone in my cramped little cubicle at the flooring mill, so I told Chris not to call me at work. If she had an overwhelming urge to whisper steamy sweet nothings into my ear during the day, I wanted to be able to collect them to savor at my leisure in the evening.

Friday was Christmas Eve, and I made it a housewarming at my new apartment. I invited Chris and McGerk—my only two friends—and told McGerk to bring a date. He accepted the invitation but wasn't bringing anyone, claiming he didn't know a woman who looked good enough to be seen in my fancy new place.

Against McGerk's advice—he'd encouraged me to chop one down in the woods at no cost—I bought a Christmas tree off a lot, put it up next to the fireplace, and decorated it. My well-used credit card also financed fireplace logs, hors d'oeuvres, eggnog, and three steak dinners with all the trimmings to be delivered by a local restaurant promptly at seven o'clock.

McGerk arrived first, decked out in a clean, woolen plaid shirt and pressed Levis, formal dress for him. Most of the grease had been scrubbed from his hands and face, his hair was neatly combed, and he'd even made a halfhearted attempt to trim the stubble on his cheeks.

Chris carried in a large tote bag instead of a purse. I knew it contained her personal things for spending the night, and I got excited just thinking about it. We exchanged a fervent kiss at the door.

Not having seen the apartment before, Chris whistled man-style. "Wow, software consulting must pay pretty good."

McGerk quipped sarcastically, "Yessir, it's an honor fer me t'be in the company of such a financial genius."

I broke out the eggnog, and we sipped it as we munched on hors d'oeuvres of shrimp, smoked salmon, and deviled eggs.

After a candlelight dinner, we sat in the living room, listening to Christmas music on my newly acquired CD player. McGerk performed magic with the logs, quickly getting a roaring fire going.

I reached under the tree and pulled out a gag gift for McGerk. It was a bottle of aftershave lotion and everyone thought it was hilarious. I also had gifts under the tree for Chris, but I planned to wait until we were alone to give them to her. I was congratulating myself on how great the evening was going and how it promised to become even better once McGerk left, when the doorbell chimed.

I opened the door; Paul and Edna Jarvi were stomping snow from their boots onto my door mat.

"MERRY CHRISTMAS, Joe," Aunt Edna pealed, handing me a brightly wrapped gift as she bustled in. "We haven't seen you in weeks and thought maybe you were spending Christmas Eve all alone in your new place."

Edna gasped as she took in the apartment. "Oh, my, how beautiful! Paul, willya look at this place."

Paul looked around critically. "How kin ya afford all this on that salary they pay ya at the flooring mill?"

I interrupted quickly. "You know Kippy McGerk of course, but I want to introduce you to my friend, Christine Arquette . . . "

I finished the introductions and hastily led Edna and Paul into the bedroom on the pretext of showing them the rest of the apartment.

Once in there, I spoke quickly and quietly. "I didn't tell you, but I had some Digitek stock from an employee profit-sharing plan. I intended to hang onto it but decided to sell some in order to buy this PC for my writing."

I gestured toward my PC in the corner of the bedroom. Edna gingerly touched the keyboard with her finger and quickly withdrew it, fearful of electric shocks or whatever computers do to people who don't understand them.

"Then I figured, what the heck, I'll sell it all and get a better place to live with enough cash left over to see me through until I can get on my feet with the book. So you see, I wasn't exactly broke when I got here."

I'm surprised you're runnin' around with that McGerk," Paul said. "He's good with cars, but I hear he spends all his free time down at that Wild Goose Bar—a real dive if there ever was one."

"No kidding? The Wild Goose Bar, huh?" I exclaimed. "It just goes to show that you can never tell about people."

Later on, Chris and I lay in the darkness of my new bedroom, happily exhausted.

Chris chuckled. "Your uncle apparently doesn't know what software consulting pays. His comment about your not being able to afford this place was pretty funny."

I nodded. "I didn't tell anyone but you about my actual position at the flooring mill. You know how small towns are. If the word gets out that they're paying big bucks for a consultant, the union people could get nasty about raises at the next round of contract talks."

Chris put her head on my chest. "Good thinking. I like smart and capable men—and *one* smart and capable man in particular."

I fell asleep realizing that I was rapidly becoming expert at snapping lies off the tip of my tongue at a moment's notice.

5

hen I arrived home from the flooring mill on the fifth of January, the credit-card statement from the Hematite First National Bank was waiting in the mailbox. I expected it, of course, but I'd been so totally preoccupied with the excitement of my new life that I hadn't given it much thought.

The envelope was crammed with page after page of charges. I looked at the total on the last page.

No, c'mon, that couldn't possibly be correct.

I added up the charges on my pocket calculator and then added them up again. It was correct.

I was working on my third Budweiser at the Wild Goose when McGerk arrived and took the stool I'd saved for him.

"I'm in serious trouble," I said.

"Now what?"

I pushed the credit-card statement over to him. McGerk looked at the total and whistled.

"On my salary, I can't even make the minimum monthly payment,"

I said.

"Jus' send 'em a li'l somethin'. They'll take anything they kin get."

"But take another look. The balance owed is just thirty-four dollars under the new extended limit they put on the account. I can charge thirty-four dollars and that's it, no more. And what about my new rent? I just figured it out. I can't afford that either. I'll be evicted. What'll Chris say when I try to sneak her into the YMCA on Friday nights?"

"Tell 'er the truth—yer just a starving writer, workin' at the flooring mill t'make ends meet."

"Are you kidding? After what I told her? If she finds out that I've been lying to her, she'll drop me like a hot rock."

"There's other fish in th'sea," McGerk replied cheerfully, waving his hand toward a group of women at a nearby table wearing Green Bay Packer sweatshirts and drinking beer. "In fact, some of 'em *expect* to be lied to."

"You don't understand. I've fallen in *love* with Chris."

McGerk frowned, trying to comprehend the enormity of that statement. "Y'mean *real* love? Now whyd'ja go an' do a thing like that for?"

"I couldn't help it. That's how I got into this fix."

The conversation was depressing. We had a few more Budweisers, and when McGerk switched over to the house whiskey, I joined him. We continued to drink in silence.

During the third whiskey, McGerk said, "You ain't the only one with money problems. I've gotten in pretty deep myself."

"Oh?"

"You ain't been over to th'garage in awhile. I took delivery on one of them fancy automatic engine analyzers—all kinds a li'l knobs an' them computer screens. Cost a bundle, but I hadda get one. All them new garages up on th'highway got 'em, an' I been losin' customers t'those guys fer years. People nowadays think that if ya don' have all that high-tech equipment to tune their car with, ya don' know what th'hell yer doin'."

McGerk motioned to the bartender with his empty glass. "So I owe all this money fer that gawdamned machine, an' I'm *still* losin' customers. If I don't do sumthin pretty quick, I'm gonna haf'ta shut down. Won't be able t'pay *my* rent either."

We sipped our whiskeys and gloomily listened to the juke box. Young millionaire country-western artists were singing their hearts out about problems they probably knew nothing about.

"There's one way *both* of us kin get outta this," McGerk said quietly.

"Oh? I'd like to hear it."

"You an' me are in a helluva fix—we both need money, right?"

"Right."

He lowered his voice even further. "Okay, so we knock over a bank."

I laughed. "McGerk, you're gettin' wacked on this cheap whiskey. I'm gonna go home while I can still remember where I live." I started to get off the stool.

He grabbed my arm in a vise-like grip. "I'm serious. Been thinkin' 'bout this a long time. It's *foolproof*, but I need a partner."

I tried to peel his fingers off my arm, but he had a firm hold. "You *are* drunk. Look, maybe I'll see you tomorrow night if my head is okay by then."

McGerk finally let go of my arm. "Think I'm drunk, huh? I'll pick ya up at th'flooring mill at noon tomorrow—cold sober. I'll show ya how it kin be done."

❄

I was too hungover the next day to object to going along when McGerk—disgustingly clear-eyed—arrived at the flooring mill at noon. I got in the truck and rolled the window down, not caring where McGerk went so long as he drove fast enough to keep the icy fresh air flowing across my throbbing head.

He headed north through downtown Ishpeming, turned onto Highway 41, and pulled into the parking lot of the Hematite First National Bank.

I sat up straight when he stopped. "*This* is the bank you want to rob?"

"It's—whaddaya call it—ironic," McGerk said. "*Your* bank's the one we're gonna hit. We take their money, and then ya pay off their credit card with part of yer share."

"McGerk, are you still drunk?" I whispered, even though we were still sitting in his truck. "Did you pour whiskey on your Wheaties this morning? *We're* not gonna hit *any* bank. I'm getting nervous as hell just sitting here talking about it."

But he wasn't drunk, and he wasn't kidding. "Have you ever robbed a bank?" I asked.

"Nope," McGerk said innocently.

"Then you're absolutely stone crazy. This may be a small town in the U.P. woods, but they've got police here and the State Police are just down the highway. They'd nail us before we even got out of the parking lot."

McGerk's bristly face expanded into a broad smile. "That's the beauty of th'plan—the getaway."

"Oh? How're we gonna get away?" I couldn't believe I was using the word 'we.'

"Snowmobiles."

"SNOWMOBILES?"

McGerk pointed through the windshield. "Whaddaya see out

there?"

"Nothing but woods."

"Tha's right—woods. We make our getaway on snowmobiles through the woods."

"Snowmobiles through the woods? McGerk, I've never been on a snowmobile in my *life*. In fact, I've never even been in the *woods*." My voice began to rise. "That's your bright idea? And you want *me* as a partner? Take me back to the flooring mill."

McGerk started up the truck. "Any damn fool kin learn to ride a snowmobile. An' travelin' through the woods is easy, long as ya don't panic. It'll work, I tell ya. Come over t'my place tonight. I'll fill ya in on more of the details."

6

*A*s I thought about it throughout the afternoon, McGerk's preposterous bank-robbery-with-snowmobiles scheme began to take on a certain grim fascination. Not because I had any intention of going along with it, mind you, but I was intrigued with finding out what kind of foolproof plan he had cooked up. Chris was teaching that night, and in my depressed state, being alone had no appeal. So I went over to McGerk's house. If nothing else, his cockamamie scheme would provide enough comic relief to cheer me up.

I sat down on the sofa and accepted a bottle of Bud. "I'm just gonna have one beer and then leave."

"Lemme tell ya how I come t'think 'bout this," McGerk began. "One Friday morning last winter—February, I think it wuz—I drove my snowmobile over to th'Hematite Bank t'cash a check. Got there 'bout nine fifteen, and the armored truck wuz parked outside—bringin' in cash. I stood at one of th'teller's windows while they were unloadin' it—haulin' all of them canvas sacks into th'bank.

"Arne Laxso, the manager, was takin' th'money out'a the sacks. Bundles of fifties, twennies, and tens—a hundred in each stack. I could see real good 'cuz he was right behind my teller, countin' th'stacks and puttin' 'em in a big metal box on a cart. While Laxso wuz countin', I wuz keepin' track in my head. There wuz over two hundred grand there."

That surprised me. "Two hundred thousand dollars in *cash*? In that little bank?"

"That's right. The bank needs lots'a money on Fridays. Everybody comes in t'cash their checks.

"Anyway, Laxso finished countin' th'money, put his initials on sum forms, and a teller wheeled the cart into th'inner vault. I could still see th'cart and th'money box though. They're supposed t'keep that inner vault locked up, but fer sum reason they leave the vault door wide open during the day. Jus' careless, I think. "

I interrupted. "Oh, I see. You're going to charge into the bank, wheel the cart out the front door, and throw this big metal cash box on the back of your snowmobile? You'd better be careful that it doesn't tip over while you're making your getaway."

I laughed at my own remark. Snowmobiles looked to me like expensive mechanical toys for grownups to play with. The mental image of using them in a bank robbery was funny as hell.

McGerk got to his feet. "C'mon, lemme show ya sumthin'."

He led me out to the garage and turned on an overhead light. A single-axle trailer with a tarp-covered load sat beneath the bare bulb. McGerk untied the tarp and pulled it off. For the first time I saw a snowmobile really close up. The machine looked a lot bigger than the ones I'd seen putt-putting over the snow next to the highways.

"Go ahead, push it off th'trailer," McGerk challenged.

I leaned hard against the snowmobile. It wouldn't budge.

"Sled weighs over five hundred fifty pounds," he said.

"Sled?"

"That's whut they call snowmobiles."

The chassis—a fiery "MACH 1" emblem on both sides—was bullet-shaped like an Indy race car. Wide skis were attached to the undercarriage with a coil suspension similar to that used on automobiles. The engine fed power to a heavy rubber track at the rear.

McGerk returned from the kitchen and handed me a fresh Bud.

"This thing moves across the snow on that track?" I asked.

He nodded.

"And you want to use it on a getaway? Doesn't look very fast to me."

McGerk pointed at the gauges between the handlebars. "Look at th'speedometer."

The top reading on the speedometer was one hundred miles per hour.

I laughed. "I don't believe it. That's a manufacturer's gimmick."

"It actually goes faster'n that. I souped it up a li'l."

"Are you trying to tell me that this thing goes over a hundred miles an hour?"

"Yep. Wouldn't use this machine fer th'job, though—too easy to trace. We steal a couple."

"From where?"

"Snowmobilers from downstate leave 'em in motel parking lots overnight alla time. Y'take yer pick. I kin hot-wire a sled in fifteen seconds."

"Let's talk about the robbery. What about bank guards?"

"Bank robberies ain't that big a problem up here. None of the banks have guards. That's why we won't need guns."

"I'm glad to hear that, but how're you going to get the bank to give you the money?"

"Ya jus' give th'teller a note sayin' you gotta gun in your jacket. Bank people are trained not t'take any chances. After all, th'money's insured. Worst that kin happen is they don't give ya th'money an' they start makin' a fuss. Nobody's armed, so y'just turn around, walk out like nuthin' happened, an' we take off on th'sleds."

By now I'd finished my second beer. "It's a small town; they'll recognize us. Not only that, every bank's got surveillance cameras."

McGerk dug into a cardboard box in the corner, brought out a large, black *Star Wars*-type helmet, and put it on. It covered his entire head with a sloping visor hinged on each side and slits around the mouth area for breathing and talking.

"Snowmobile helmet," he explained. "During th'winter, snowmobilers walk around all over town with helmets on. Shopkeepers are used to 'em. The tellers'll jus' think yer a tourist wantin' t'cash traveler's checks or sumthin'."

"You can still see into this visor," I said. "They'll recognize you."

McGerk produced a ski mask and put it on. He took the helmet, pulled it down over the mask, and faced me. I wouldn't have had a clue who he was.

He added, "We steal helmets at th'same time we steal the snowmobiles. Even th'gloves, jackets, and pants."

I wasn't about to press McGerk for details on how he intended to steal someone's snowmobile pants. "Now, I don't know much about snow, but I know you leave tracks in it. The police could follow us on snowmobiles."

"The state police got sleds, but they share 'em with the Department of Natural Resource guys who usually keep 'em out on th'groomed trails. Besides, we won't be leavin' tracks fer very long."

"Why not?"

"Cause we pull the job during a snowstorm."

"A *snowstorm*? Let me get this straight, we knock over a bank—which, of course, I've never done—make our getaway into the woods—which I've never been in—on stolen snowmobiles—which I've never driven, and all of this in a *snowstorm*?"

McGerk grinned broadly and nodded.

I headed for the garage door. "It's been a lot of fun listening to your plan, but count me out. I've got to go home and try to figure out how to get myself out of this money mess."

"That's the whole point," McGerk insisted. "How *are* ya gonna get out? You could declare bankruptcy, I guess. But ya still gotta find a cheaper place t'live an' cut way back on expenses. An' sooner or later, you'll haf'ta level with Chris. As y'said yerself, she'll be pissed off 'bout all them lies.

"But if y'get yer hands on sum quick cash, not only kin ya pay off th'credit card, you'd have plenty left over. With a hundred grand, you kin keep the fancy apartment an' yerself in nice clothes fer *years*. Chris'd never know a thing. Ya'd still have her helpin' ya to get that book done. I bet you could even quit yer job at th'mill an' write full-time."

"Listen, if this's such a great plan, why do you need me? Why not do it by yourself and keep *all* the cash?"

"It's a two-man job. Fer one thing, a snowmobile doesn' have any real storage space. It'll take th'two of us to carry off all that cash."

What he said struck a chord. *All that cash.*

"But why *me*?" I asked. "You certainly must know guys around here that have a helluva lot of experience running snowmobiles around the woods."

"Yup, sure do, an' I thought 'bout that. But I don't want t'hook up with sum yahoo just wantin' a li'l spendin' money. He'll be spreadin' it all around town th'day after the robbery. You need th'money bad."

McGerk sensed that I was beginning to waver. "C'mon back in th'house an' have another beer."

I sat down on the sofa, sipping a fresh Bud while McGerk continued his story.

"I went back th'next two Fridays. Them armored-car guys were always there, johnny-on-the-spot at nine-fifteen. The cash wuz always left in that metal box on the table cart in the vault with th'door wide open.

"Then, on the last Friday, when I left th'bank, I jumped on the sled an'—jus' fer th'hell of it—cut it loose into the woods. I wuz out of sight of th'bank in less'n ten seconds."

I mentally pictured the distance. "*Ten seconds*? I don't believe that."

McGerk laughed. "I see I'll haf'ta take ya fer a ride on my sled."

"You said bank robberies aren't a problem up here. There must be a good reason. Nobody gets away with it, right?"

McGerk nodded. "That's pretty much true. Th'bozos who've tried it stuck to the roads, figurin' on makin' a run for it. They got nailed. But there's been a coupl'a bank jobs in the U.P. where they never caught th'guys. That's 'cause they'd planned th'getaway well in advance, stayed off the roads, an' knew their way 'round th'woods."

"You're really convinced that we can go into that bank, give the teller a note, walk out with two hundred thousand in cash, and escape on two snowmobiles into the woods?"

McGerk nodded.

"In a *snowstorm*?" The idea frightened the hell out of me.

He nodded again.

I tried to remember how many beers I'd drunk. It wasn't enough. "This is the most hairbrained, suicidal plan I've ever heard. Have you got any whiskey around here?"

McGerk shook his head. "No gettin' drunk tonight. Tomorrow we're gonna introduce ya t'snowmobilin'."

❄

7

*A*t three o'clock the next day, Friday, I told the office manager at the mill that I felt sick and was going home. Fifteen minutes later McGerk showed up at my apartment, pulling the flat-bed trailer behind his pickup. The tarp-covered MACH 1 looked like a hooded falcon waiting to be freed.

We drove for twenty minutes, first toward Marquette, then south along some road I'd never been on before. Winter was in full force now. Snow-laden evergreens lined the road, but only the tops were visible since county plows had piled the snow six feet and higher along the roadsides.

I was tense. Merely being with McGerk in his pickup truck heading out for a snowmobile ride meant that I was going along with this crazy idea. *A bank robbery!* I'd never even stolen a candy bar when I was a kid.

We pulled off onto a much narrower secondary road, and McGerk stopped the truck a quarter-mile in. He tripped a latch near the hitch, and the trailer tilted backward, the rear end touching the snow. Then he pulled the tarp from the snowmobile and pressed the electric starter. The MACH 1 coughed and snarled to life, emitting clouds of oily exhaust.

McGerk pulled heavy snowmobile clothing and two helmets from the pickup's cross-bed storage compartment. He held out a pair of thickly padded trousers with suspenders and a slick, multi-colored padded jacket.

"Put these on. It's below zero and it'll be cold as hell on th'sled."

Wearing long johns under my wool pants and a sweater beneath the Nautica jacket, I was still sweating from the truck heater. "I'll be okay with what I've got on."

"Suit yerself," McGerk said, getting dressed. He hopped onto the snowmobile seat and revved up the engine. Without warning, the MACH 1 scrambled off the trailer onto the snow. He put his helmet on and handed me the other one. I pushed it down over my ears and immediately felt claustrophobic.

I climbed on behind McGerk, not sure what to do with my hands and feet.

McGerk opened his visor, turned, and yelled to me. "This sled's a racer—not designed fer two people—but we'll manage. Just put yer feet up an' grab hold a me."

I balanced my feet on the narrow aluminum runners and tried to wrap my arms around McGerk's waist, but my gloves kept sliding around on his slick jacket. The back support of the short seat burrowed into my spine.

We started off, bouncing along the snow until we came to a groomed snowmobile trail in the trees. McGerk turned onto the trail, picking up speed. We proceeded south under an archway of snow-covered tree limbs.

It was a beautiful setting, but I wasn't enjoying it. The sharp, sub-zero air penetrated my clothing, and I was growing painfully cold.

The trail emerged from the trees onto a long snow-covered meadow. I looked over McGerk's shoulder, noting that the trail straightened out for a mile or more toward a distant clump of spruce.

The MACH 1 let loose with an unearthly grinding shriek, bucked up—skis in the air—and leapt forward. My boots slid off the runners, and I nearly lost my grip on McGerk's waist.

The acceleration was frightening. More alarming, the wind was tearing through my clothes like millions of icy knives. I yelled at McGerk to slow down, but with his helmet on he couldn't hear me above the engine noise. I caught a glimpse of the speedometer—the needle was registering eighty-five. I'd never even driven my BMW at that speed.

The MACH 1 was now planing across the snow, smoothing out the ride. I took a chance—removed my right hand from McGerk's waist and opened my helmet visor so I could yell at him again to slow down.

That was a monumental mistake. The closed visor made the helmet aerodynamically efficient with air flowing smoothly around it. With the visor open, the air hit me squarely in the face, instantly numbing my nose, eyes, and mouth. It whistled around inside the helmet invading my ears. My whole head was freezing.

I put a glove up to the helmet to push the visor back down into place. It wouldn't move. Panic-stricken, I frantically slapped at the visor with one glove, all the while screaming at McGerk.

The MACH 1 slowed down as we reached the end of the mile-long straightaway, yet we didn't stop. McGerk immediately whipped the snowmobile off the trail, making a wide turn onto the meadow to head back to the truck. We shot back down the straightaway trail, and I had no recourse but to plaster my open helmet firmly against his back.

We pulled up to the truck, the sled's engine idling fretfully. McGerk popped his visor open, his breath escaping in puffy clouds. "Still think we can't get away from th'bank quick enough?"

"Ghaaahhh." I had no feeling in my tongue.

"Ya shouldn't keep th'visor open. "You kin get frostbite doin' that."

"Uuhhkkk."

McGerk got off the snowmobile. "Now *you* take a turn drivin'."

I tried to tell him to go to hell, but nothing came out. All I could do was shake my head.

"Ya gotta. Remember, we haf'ta use two sleds."

I flipped McGerk an obscene gesture and staggered toward the relative warmth of the truck.

"Does that mean yer not goin' through with th'job?" McGerk called after me.

An hour later, shortly after McGerk had dropped me off, Chris arrived at my apartment with an armload of groceries to cook dinner. One of my newly implemented austerity moves was convincing her that eating at my place on weekends was more romantic than dining in restaurants.

She touched my cheek and frowned. "What happened to you? Your face is all red."

"McGerk dook me for a nomobile ride dis afernoon."

She grew concerned. "What's wrong with your voice?"

"My dongue's frozen, I dink."

"Weren't you wearing a helmet?"

"Yeah, I was . . . iss a long story."

Chris opened a can of beef broth, poured it into a mug, and heated it in the microwave. I drank it gratefully.

She began peeling and cutting up fresh vegetables at the kitchen counter, glancing at me with amusement. "You don't strike me as the type who'd take up snowmobiling."

"I'm not."

Still shaking badly, I went to the cupboard and took out the bottle of Christian Brothers brandy.

Chris prepared dinner and I sipped brandy, pondering my near-death on the snowmobile. The experience demonstrated in no uncertain terms that I wasn't cut out for McGerk's bank job. I'd never be able to pull off a high-speed getaway, *especially* in cold weather. The escape from the bank would no doubt be much further than the run we'd taken that afternoon and maybe faster—although I couldn't see how. By the time the police caught up with me—and they most certainly would—I'd have either wrapped the snowmobile around a tree or be frozen as stiff as a supermarket cod—or both. McGerk would have to pull off his get-rich-quick scheme all by himself.

"You know what we ought to do this weekend?" Chris said cheerfully. "Drive down to Green Bay tomorrow morning. I'd like to shop at those upscale stores in the mall and eat in some nice restaurants. We could stay in a hotel right downtown."

She smiled seductively, reaching over and placing a hamburger-moist hand on mine. "I get turned on just thinking about checking into a big fancy hotel with you—something we can't do here. What do you think?"

What I was thinking about was the thirty-four dollars left on my credit card.

I could just picture it—suitcases already on the bellhop's cart— the two of us standing at the front desk of a posh Green Bay hotel and the desk clerk handing the credit card back to me and saying in a polite voice. "I'm sorry, Mr. Jarvi. The computer doesn't seem to accept your card. Probably just a glitch. Perhaps you have another card . . . "

"I . . . can't do it this weekend. I have to work."

Her smile evaporated. "At the flooring mill? You've never worked on weekends before."

"I know, but they've got some problems with the budget spreadsheets . . . new computer system. I have to fix it as soon as possible."

She kept looking at me. "Are you okay?"

"What?"

"Is everything okay with you? The last few days when we've talked on the phone you've sounded . . . well, sort of preoccupied or distant, like you're not telling me something."

"Everything's fine. It's just that the work at the mill is getting hectic. It'll all be straightened out in a few weeks."

Chris wiped her hands on her apron and came around the bar. She put her arms around my neck. "Are *we* okay? I mean, you aren't getting tired of me, are you?"

A lump caught in my throat. "Tired of *you*? Are you kidding? I haven't even gotten *used* to you yet. I'll *never* get tired of you, believe me."

Chris leaned over and kissed me. "I'm sorry if it sounds like I'm prying into your affairs. During our marriage my ex lied to me all the time, and I guess I got a little paranoid after awhile. I know I don't have to worry about that anymore."

She touched my red nose lightly and clucked. "I've got a tube of skin cream in my purse. After dinner we'll put some on your face. And do me a favor—don't take up snowmobiling. It's dangerous. People get killed on them all the time."

"I can believe that."

"We'll put the Green Bay trip on hold. Maybe next weekend, okay?"

I nodded.

Chris took off her apron. "While dinner's in the oven, I'm going to take a quick shower."

As soon as she closed the bathroom door, I picked up the phone and dialed McGerk's number. I'd just run out of options.

❄

8

*C*hris left for Marquette the next morning to allow me to—as I led her to believe—go to the flooring mill to fix the spreadsheet problem.

As soon as she took off, I drove to McGerk's place. He was out in the garage making adjustments to the MACH 1's engine.

"Glad ya changed yer mind. Givin' 'er a tuneup. I noticed it wuz a li'l sluggish yesterday."

"You're joking, right?"

"No. When I got 'er up to eighty-five, it started t'act a li'l sluggish. I think I got 'er fixed, though."

"Listen—I've never driven anything but a car and most of that on nice, smooth California freeways. There's no way in hell I can drive one of these things eighty-five miles an hour across the snow."

"Won't haf'ta go anywheres near that fast. When we pull th'job, everybody in the bank'll be caught so flatfooted they won't even *think* about chasin' us. We'll be in th'woods an' gone before they know whut happened. An' don't worry, *anybody* kin drive one a these sleds. It's simple."

After my one disastrous ride, I'd become a true believer in snowmobile gear. I put on the heavily padded trousers, jacket, and gloves while McGerk hooked the snowmobile trailer to the pickup.

We took off.

This time we drove to Teal Lake, adjacent to Highway 41 between Ishpeming and the neighboring town of Negaunee. McGerk reasoned that with me at the controls, a little more open space might be a good idea.

At the east end of the lake he turned off the highway and put the truck into four-wheel drive. We crossed the snow-covered beach to the edge of the lake and stopped.

The frigid northwest wind coming off the two-mile-long lake had nothing to impede it, biting maliciously at my nose and cheeks. I hurriedly put the helmet on—visor down.

McGerk drove the MACH 1 off the trailer, explaining that the only thing I needed to know was that the right and left levers on the handlebars were the throttle and brake, respectively. "Okay," he said. "Climb on, take the controls, an' give 'er sum gas."

I sat down in the driver's position and tentatively squeezed the right hand lever. The engine roared, and the machine leapt forward like a goosed grizzly bear. My hands flew off the handlebars, and I lost my footing, nearly falling off. Without my hand on the throttle control, the snowmobile obediently stopped a few feet away.

"Too much gas too quick," McGerk advised. "At 4500 rpm th'sled starts t'move."

"It'd be nice if you explained these little things to me before I kill myself."

For a minute or two I just sat on the snowmobile, experimentally moving the handlebars back and forth and gunning the throttle as much as I dared.

McGerk climbed on behind me. "I think we're ready fer a go at it."

I pulled my visor down and carefully squeezed the throttle, watching the rpm's creep up. Finally, the MACH 1 lurched forward. I pressed the throttle with more authority, and the snowmobile gained speed. For a few minutes I was fully occupied trying to steer and steady the throttle at the same time. Then I began to get the hang of it. Bravely, I got the machine up to thirty miles an hour, and we headed for the middle of the lake.

For the next half hour I piloted the snowmobile around Teal Lake, gaining confidence. It reminded me of learning to ride a bicycle. Once I got over the initial fear, it was fun.

"Yer still too pokey," McGerk yelled.

I nodded. No problem. The sled picked up speed, and the cold wind began beating at my body, but I was wearing much warmer clothing now and it felt good. I continued to accelerate. Teal Lake—long, white, and flat like the Bonneville Salt Flats—invited speed.

As it did yesterday, the MACH 1 rose up at the higher velocity and began planing on the snow, the engine wailing like a banshee.

I felt utterly exhilarated and shouted, just for the hell of it, although inside the helmet it sounded like a muffled yelp.

The speedometer read sixty miles an hour. I pressed the throttle even harder.

We were heading for the west end of the lake, which narrowed significantly into an inlet to the north of Ishpeming. I hadn't been over there during the earlier runs that afternoon, but one part of a frozen lake was just like any other. Or so I thought.

The speedometer registered seventy. Damn—fast as driving on the California freeways. Maybe after we pull the bank job I'll buy one of these things.

McGerk punched me hard on the shoulder and pointed straight ahead. He yelled something, but the engine noise was too loud.

At first I couldn't see anything out of the ordinary, the light was flat in the overcast sky.

Then I saw why McGerk was getting so excited. The prevailing winter winds whipping down a small gully at the north shore of the lake had pushed snow onto the ice—a *lot* of snow. At this narrow part of the lake the snowdrift extended from shore to shore. We were a hundred yards away and heading right at it—at seventy miles an hour.

"BRAKES!" McGerk screamed into the side of my helmet.

Omigawd—which hand is the brakes?

McGerk whacked my left arm to jog my memory. I squeezed the left-hand lever—*HARD*.

The MACH 1 shuddered and fishtailed, trying to stop, but was still going about thirty miles an hour when we hit the drift.

With monstrous, bone-jarring impacts, the snowmobile bounced up the sloping snow. It alternately reared up, plunged down, and spun like an enraged Brahma bull, splashing a huge sheet of snow up over the windshield. The skis twisted violently, wrenching the handlebars out of my grip. McGerk's hands pushed hard against my waist as he threw himself clear.

The sled bucked brutally one more time before tossing me into the air.

I hit the deep crest of the snowdrift. Dense snow rammed into my helmet as the visor slammed open. I couldn't breathe. I twisted the helmet off and gasped in the cold air. The MACH 1's engine was grumbling a short distance away—unbelievably, still running. I tried to get up, but my arms and legs wouldn't cooperate. Everything hurt.

McGerk's boots crunched through the snow. He trotted on past me and knelt down next to the MACH 1 lying on its side some twenty yards away.

"We could'a made it if ya hadn't let go of th'handlebars. *Never* let go of th'handlebars."

McGerk inspected his beloved machine. "No damage, I guess. Looks t'be okay." He carefully righted the snowmobile while I lay patiently in the snow waiting my turn.

Chris was due back from Marquette late that afternoon to spend the night. I had calculated that I'd be home long before she arrived and even concocted a story about problems with the mill spreadsheets to amuse her.

But the snowmobile accident on Teal Lake wasn't a part of the equation. Time was spent on the ice determining that I had no broken bones. Then, slowly and carefully I hoisted myself into the truck and removed the padded trousers and jacket. It took forever to drive home from McGerk's place. My right leg didn't want to rise up to use the brake pedal. Several minutes were spent carefully removing myself from the car and inching into the apartment. By that time I was only five minutes ahead of Chris.

I let her in, and she hugged me enthusiastically as we kissed. I groaned in pain.

"What's the matter?"

I hobbled into the living room, carefully lowering myself onto the sofa. "I fell on the icy sidewalk at the mill today."

"You look like you're in real pain."

"Yeah, well . . . I'm pretty sore."

"You know what's good for that?" she said. "A nice hot bath. Take off your clothes and I'll run the water in the tub."

After stripping down, I limped into the bathroom. Chris did a double take when she saw my body. "Ohmigawd—you got *that* falling on the sidewalk? Where did you fall from—a second-story window?"

Angry bruises liberally covered my legs, arms, and back. It was a scary sight.

"Didn't the mill put sand on the sidewalk?"

I carefully lowered myself into the hot water. "Uh . . . I guess they must've missed a spot."

"Worker's compensation covers that. First thing Monday morning, go in and see the nurse or whoever takes care of on-the-job accidents at the flooring mill."

"Well, I don't want to create any problems for them." This was getting complicated.

Chris glared and pursed her lips, pressing a hot washcloth against a nasty-looking spot on my shoulder. "It's no problem for the mill. They have to carry insurance for that sort of thing. You need to see a doctor to determine if there are any fractures. Doctors and lab tests cost money. That's why you'd better talk to the people at the mill."

I closed my eyes and settled down in the hot water, trying not to think about it.

9

*T*he following afternoon the phone rang.

"Has she gone?" McGerk asked.

"Yeah, an hour ago."

"Good. We got work t'do today. First, we gotta take a sled ride before it gets dark."

"TODAY? I have to ride that damned thing again *today*? I'm so stiff I won't even be able to get *on* it!"

"Lissen, we don' have all the time in th'world, ya know. If the weather conditions're right, we pull th'job off this week."

"This week? I haven't even heard all the details of the job yet."

"I'll give ya details later. Pick ya up in ten minutes."

I hobbled over to the front door to get my boots on. The shape I was in, it would take me at least ten minutes to get dressed.

At first I didn't recognize McGerk's pickup, with a big BOSS snowplow mounted on the front end. Many truck owners use these plows to clear snow from their private roadways during the long U.P. winters. McGerk's plow was so large that the blade covered the truck's grill and headlights. Auxiliary headlights attached to the ends of metal conduit peeked up over the blade.

We went east out of Ishpeming, trailering the MACH 1. In the midst of a maze of unmarked county roads, we stopped at a small two-rut trail completely clogged with snow. McGerk flipped a toggle switch next to the steering wheel, and with a whine, the snowplow lowered itself into position. We proceeded slowly on the narrow trail, pushing the deep snow to one side.

"Where the hell are we going?" I asked.

"We're gonna check out th'getaway route."

"Getaway route? You mean we're actually somewhere near the bank? You had me fooled."

Two hundred yards down the trail, we came to a wide meadow surrounded by dense woods. McGerk stopped and disconnected the trailer. For the next few minutes he worked the plow, clearing an area large enough to turn the truck around.

Then he started up the MACH 1 and drove it off the trailer. We donned our snowmobile gear and with McGerk driving, headed into the woods.

McGerk had to proceed slowly, looking for openings through the trees and underbrush. More than once, the snowmobile got stuck in deep snow and we both had to get off to free it.

"You can't be serious about making a snowmobile getaway through this stuff," I shouted over the engine noise.

"It'll work," McGerk replied. "I once knew this area purty good—use'ta deer hunt in here—but that wuz years ago. I'm checkin' it out today 'cause I don't wanna be scootin' through here after th'job, not knowin' where there might be dead trees or rocks underneath th'snow."

I sat on the back of the snowmobile, ducking evergreen branches.

"It's crazy!" I yelled.

"No, it ain't."

Some thirty minutes later, we suddenly emerged from the woods at the highway, directly across from the Hematite First National Bank. McGerk had known exactly where he was every minute.

We turned the snowmobile around and headed back into the woods along the trail we'd just broken. McGerk gunned the MACH 1 now, and while I still had to duck the occasional branch, we fairly shot back to the meadow in a fraction of the time it took to get to the highway.

Back in the truck, we headed toward Ishpeming. McGerk still hadn't explained enough of the details of the robbery, and I had to know more. "Okay, so that's the getaway route. Let's hear the rest of it."

He nodded. "Before daylight, on th'day we pull the job, we steal two sleds from one of the motel parkin' lots. Them downstate snowmobilers leave 'em all nicely wrapped up on th'back of their trailers overnight. Usually even have the trailer hitched up to their pickups. An' they often leave their helmets an' cold-weather gear right in the truck cab. Handy. We jus' take th'whole thing."

"We steal the truck and trailer, too?"

"Why not? Auto theft is piddlin' stuff compared t'robbin' a bank. We take the stolen rig an' my truck up to that meadow. 'Bout nine-thirty we drive the sleds through th'woods to th'bank like we just did. Pull the job, shoot back to the meadow, transfer th'money into the cross-bed box on my truck, leave everything else there, an' drive back into Ishpeming.

"Nobody goes into that area in th'winter. With a decent snow, the stolen truck, trailer, an' sleds'll be covered up, an' the cops may not find that stuff till the spring thaw. Even if they finally get organized an' try followin' our escape route with sleds, the snowstorm will've covered our tracks an' they'll have a helluva time."

"We drive right back to Ishpeming?"

"Yep. Return to th'scene of th'crime—nobody'll expect that. We jus' go on home like nuthin' happened."

McGerk glanced at me. "Whaddaya think?"
"It just might work."

At McGerk's apartment we moved on to the next step.
"*I* have to write the holdup note to give to the teller?"
"Hell, you're th'writer, ain'cha?" McGerk said. "If I write it, somebody'll remember th'bad English, an' I'll get picked up right away. I'll tell ya what'cha gotta say, an' you put it in the right words."

McGerk dumped a stack of old *Mining Journal* newspapers down on the living-room floor. "We don' wanna give 'em a sample of yer handwritin', so ya cut words outta th'newspaper."

I looked skeptically at the stack of *Mining Journals*. "They'll trace the print font and know it came from the local paper."

McGerk grunted. "So what? Everybody gets the *Mining Journal*—even th'tourists. That don't narrow down anything."

I took the pertinent information from McGerk, carefully composing text for the teller's note, all the while making editorial changes to get it just right.

McGerk finally got impatient. "Fer crissakes, quit already. This is a *holdup* note. We ain't trying fer a lit'rachure prize."

When I was finished, the note read:

THIS IS A ROBBERY. REMAIN CALM AND NO ONE WILL GET HURT. GO QUIETLY INTO THE VAULT AND WHEEL OUT THE CART WITH THE METAL CASHBOX. EMPTY THE CASHBOX AND THE CASH FROM THE TELLERS' DRAWERS— LARGE DENOMINATIONS ONLY—INTO THE KNAPSACKS. DO NOT ACTIVATE THE ALARMS.

WE HAVE HIDDEN GUNS AND WON'T HESITATE
TO USE THEM IF THERE'S TROUBLE.

I held the sheet up for McGerk's inspection. "Looks pretty good, huh?"

McGerk looked over my shoulder. "Change the last sentence to say 'I have a hidden gun an' won't hesitate t'use it if there's trouble.'"

I was puzzled. "We want the teller to think we *both* have guns, don't we?"

"She won't see two of us. I'll be th'outside man."

"*Outside* man? What do you mean, you'll be the outside man?"

"I'll be in the parkin' lot, lookin' after the sleds—keep the engines runnin', that sort'a thing. After th'robbery every second counts, an' we can't afford t'fool around startin' up a cranky engine. Besides, I know every cop up here by sight, even when they're not in uniform. If I see sumpthin' that looks funny, I'll come right inta the bank an' get ya."

I was dumbfounded. "Do you mean to say that you expect *me* to hold up that bank *alone*?"

"Nuthin' to it," McGerk reassured me. "Remember, I studied th'whole thing fer weeks. We pull up a li'l after ten in the morning. The armored truck'll have been there an' gone. Maria Grazzelli'll be the only teller. Th'other tellers'll be on their ten o'clock coffee break. It's a slack time—a good chance there won't be any customers in the bank. Arne Laxso is usually in his office in th'back, so he won' know whut's happenin'. Ya only got one unarmed woman t'worry about. Jus' hand her the note and the two duffel bags."

I jumped off the sofa and began pacing. "*You* be the inside man if it's so easy!"

McGerk sneered. "An' have *you* tendin' the sleds an' watchin' out fer cops? Now, *that's* risky."

"McGerk, I'm just a downsized computer jockey trying to be a writer. The only reason I'm in on this is that you talked me into it. What the hell do I know about robbing banks?"

"Who d'ya think *I* am? Jesse James?"

"I'm not gonna be in there alone, McGerk."

"Ya haf'ta. There's another reason I gotta stay outside."

"What's that?"

"Th'teller who'll be in th'bank—Maria Grazzelli—I used'ta go out with her."

"You used to date the teller? That's just great—the thrill of holding up a bank in a small town. But we'll have helmets and ski masks on. She won't recognize you. "

"Still too risky. She knows me pretty well. Would you take a chance handin' Chris a holdup note wearin' a helmet an' ski mask? All it would take is Maria gettin' a glimpse of my eyes. She'd know me."

"Well, crissake, let's pick another bank."

McGerk shook his head. "I cased this one down to th'last detail. We know the delivery schedule fer th'money. They leave the inner vault door open. Already checked out th'getaway route. We don't have time t'do all that fer another bank."

We argued at length, but McGerk stood firm. I finally gave in and clipped the words out of the old newspapers and pasted them onto a blank sheet of paper. McGerk thoughtfully provided snug-fitting rubber gloves so I wouldn't leave fingerprints on the note.

"Ya did good," McGerk said, inspecting the final product. "Now we wait fer a nice Friday-mornin' snowstorm."

❄

10

*L*ook at that front over western Oregon," I said to McGerk, pointing at the weather map on the TV screen. "It's going to reach us by Friday morning."

"Nah, that system's gonna slide south of us--probably hit Milwaukee an' Chicago--an' leave us high an' dry."

"But the jet-stream pattern they had up there ten minutes ago--it'll carry that front right over us."

McGerk sneered. "No, dummy, ain'cha been listenin'? That jet stream's gonna get depressed by that high pressure system sittin' over Thunder Bay. Gonna push all that snow right into Milwaukee. Now, why don'cha put a sock in it an' get us another beer."

On the last Wednesday in January our nerves were wound tight waiting for a Friday-morning snowstorm. January had brought plenty of snow, but for some reason it always arrived early in the week. Every Friday—armored-car day—dawned clear and dry. Our holdup was on hold.

Since McGerk didn't have cable TV, he'd gotten into the habit of coming over to my place after dinner to watch the Weather Channel. We had become amateur meteorologists, spending weekday evenings sipping Budweiser while inspecting TV weather maps and sniping at each other's forecasting.

We discussed pulling the job without the aid of a snowstorm, but McGerk vetoed that, claiming that a heavy snowfall provided the necessary cover. Without it, he said, some hot-dog sledder might decide to chase after us along the getaway route, or the police would certainly find a tire print from McGerk's pickup if they quickly recovered the stolen truck and snowmobiles in the meadow.

I took advantage of the waiting period and practiced on the MACH 1. I was extra careful to avoid mishaps so I wouldn't have to explain any new injuries to Chris when she came over on the weekend.

The five-day local forecast flashed on the TV screen, verifying McGerk's prediction—clear and cold through Monday.

Disgruntled, he finished off his beer. "Well, that's it fer *this* Friday. You kin go back to yer writin' this weekend."

"Waiting around to rob a bank isn't compatible with writing romance."

"No? Well, at least yer gettin' in some good research fer th'love scenes, ain'cha?"

"Chris says my love scenes are cute—claims my hero behaves just like I do. I don't know if that's a compliment or an insult."

"How's yer money situation?" McGerk asked.

"Bad. I took out another loan from the Hematite Bank to pay the rent this month."

"From the *same* bank? How'ja manage that? I would'a thought they'd be after yer ass 'bout now."

"They are. They mailed me another credit-card bill with a strong letter insisting that I submit the overdue minimum amount immediately. I only got the loan because I took out a lien on my car."

"Y'think Chris is gettin' wise?" McGerk asked.

"I don't think so. If she wonders why we aren't dining out anymore or why I keep ducking that Green Bay weekend, she hasn't said anything. She seems content to come over on weekends, cook dinner, edit my manuscript, and just be with me.

"This whole thing is nuts. My life's either going to get a lot better or a hell of a lot worse, and right now it all hinges on the damned weather. I'm scared stiff of this bank job and scared even worse of what'll happen if we *don't* do it. Which brings up the point, what the hell are we gonna do if we never get snow on a Friday?"

McGerk crushed his beer can and got up to leave. He slapped my shoulder comfortingly. "Relax. Up here we get long winters an' lot'sa snow."

Late the next evening the doorbell rang.

"SURPRISE!" Chris cried out as I opened the door.

"What are you doing here on Thursday?"

"No Friday classes. There's an instructors' seminar all day tomorrow, but I'm playing hooky. I decided to give myself a long weekend with you. What's the matter, don't you want me for a long weekend?"

I pulled her into the apartment and slammed the door. We kissed at length as I unbuttoned her heavy coat.

"I know just how to get this long weekend started," I said. We both shed clothing on the way to the bedroom, not an easy task while walking and kissing.

Chris noted my obviously intense state of arousal as we got into bed.

"Take it easy," she purred. "We've got all night."

The phone rang.

"Don't answer it," Chris said.

"The damned answering machine will record the message and then keep beeping until I play it back. I don't know who it could be this time of night—probably a wrong number. I'll make it fast." I picked up the bedside phone.

"Turn on th'Weather Channel," McGerk said.

"What?"

"I jus' saw th'weather report on th'late news. That high pressure over Hudson Bay is movin'. Now there's an upper-level low comin' in right over th'lake. That big front coming in from Oregon is headed right for us now."

I was hearing the words, but they weren't sinking in. "What?" I repeated.

"Are you drunk?"

"No."

Then, McGerk sensed I wasn't alone. "Is Chris there?"

"Uh . . . yes."

"Yer gonna haf'ta feed 'er some excuse. Our Friday-morning snowstorm is due in about six hours. This is it, ol' buddy. They're talkin' about a foot of snow before noon—it's perfect. We may never getta better chance."

"Ohmigawd," I mumbled. Still grasping the phone, I swung my legs over the side of the bed onto the floor.

Chris sat up in bed. "What's wrong?"

McGerk's voice continued to crackle into my ear. "We gotta snatch a pickup, trailer, an' two sleds an' get 'em out to that meadow before th'snow gets too deep. I'll pick ya up at 5 A.M."

"No . . . no . . . uh, wait a minute. I'll come over there," I muttered.

"Okay," McGerk replied. "But be here no later'n five o'clock—five hours from now." He hung up.

"What's wrong?" Chris repeated, growing more concerned.

I was thinking fast. "Uh . . . they had a power outage at the flooring mill. One of the night-shift people thought I'd better come over and check the computers. We've got a lot of payroll information on the hard drives, and I have to back it up from floppy disks."

"When do you have to go?"

"Um . . . soon. In a few hours."

"A few *hours* from now? Why? It's the middle of the night. If you've got the data backed up on disks, can't it wait till Monday morning?" She was sitting up in bed, completely naked, and I thought seriously about calling McGerk back.

"I'd better get there as soon as I can."

"You're lying," Chris snapped.

"What?"

"Something's going on—I can tell. I began to suspect it weeks ago when you gave me that story about working the weekend I suggested going to Green Bay. You've changed. You can't seem to concentrate on anything anymore. It's even affected your writing. What is it—another woman? Can't she get to sleep without you tonight?" Chris suddenly jumped out of bed and began to dress.

"Chris, it's the truth—I've got to go over to the mill." It sounded lame, even to me.

But she was hopping mad. "I'm leaving. Call me when you're ready to tell me the truth, and then we'll talk, not before."

She stalked into the living room and began putting on her coat and boots.

Naked, I followed her. "I don't have to be over there for awhile. Come on back to bed."

Chris glanced at the effect that McGerk's phone call'd had on my libido. "Why bother?" She snapped and stomped out, slamming the door behind her.

❄

Twenty minutes later I knocked on McGerk's door.

He opened it, fully dressed. Apparently, he hadn't been able to sleep either.

"Yer early. Whad'ja do with Chris?"

"I fed her a story but she didn't buy it. She blew her stack and left. Gawd, McGerk, she thinks I'm running around with another woman."

"Ferget that fer now. Yer love life'll get a lot better once y'get some cash in yer pockets. Right now let's concentrate on the job at hand."

McGerk had amassed a large pile of gear in the middle of his living-room floor—blankets, thermos bottles, food, gas cans, and assorted tools.

He glanced at his wristwatch. "Good thing ya got here early. We kin use the extra time in case we have trouble findin' what we need. Let's load this stuff up an' get started."

11

*H*eavy snow was already falling when we began making the rounds of the motel parking lots. The snowfall helped because it diminished visibility, and the last thing we needed were witnesses. At the fourth motel McGerk spotted a rig that he liked.

He parked his truck next to a new GMC crew-cab pickup hooked up to a twin-axle trailer loaded with a pair of snowmobiles wrapped in matching brightly colored covers.

McGerk didn't waste any time. He got out, peeked into the GMC's cab, and took out a small leather case containing several rings of keys. After hurriedly inserting and testing six or seven keys in the door lock, he found one that worked. He got in and started up the engine.

Just as quickly, he jumped out and came back to his truck where I was waiting nervously.

"It's good—two helmets, jackets, pants, even duffel bags in th'back seat. You take th'GMC an' follow me."

"McGerk, I've never pulled a trailer."

"Well, I don' suppose ya ever plowed a road either, have ya? I haf'ta lead th'way with my truck, an' with this snow I'll be plowin' my way through some a them county roads. I *know* I gotta replow that li'l road into th'meadow before we kin get that GMC with the trailer an' sleds in there."

The headlights of a late-arriving motel customer cut our conversation short. We tried to act casual as he parked and walked into the front entrance, but it was certain that if we hung around there much longer, someone was bound to get suspicious.

Heart pounding, I trudged through the gathering snow over to the idling GMC and got behind the wheel.

"McGerk," I whispered loudly. "Where are the headlights and windshield wipers on this thing?"

McGerk trotted over, reached in, and turned on the lights and wipers. "We got plenty of time, so I'm gonna drive slow 'cause it's gettin' a li'l deep out here. Jus' follow me at a safe distance, an' go easy on the brakes. Ya don't wanna jackknife that trailer. Keep yer gloves on while ya drive so ya don't leave fingerprints."

"McGerk?"

"What?"

"I've got to pee."

"Forget it. Let's get outta here."

It was eerie. All I could see in the headlights were McGerk's taillights and billions of snowflakes. We were only traveling about thirty miles an hour, but I kept tapping the brakes nervously.

I had no idea how McGerk knew where he was going. There were no signs or streetlights along the confusing network of roads we were taking. It was like journeying through a dark, wooly tunnel. A few times, McGerk slowed to a stop, lowered the BOSS plow, and cleared drifting snow from the road.

Finally, stopping again, he put the plow down once more and got out of the truck and came over to me.

"This is th'road to that meadow. I'll plow an' you follow. With that trailer ya gotta swing wide to th'left before ya turn, though."

I carefully executed the turn, and we proceeded very slowly onto the narrow road, McGerk in front, plowing the way. A few times the GMC's wheels spun, but we made it in without incident. In the beam of the headlights there was absolutely no sign that we had plowed the meadow only weeks before.

McGerk switched off the engine of his pickup and climbed into the GMC with a big thermos and a paper sack.

"What do we do now?" I asked.

"Have breakfast an' wait fer daylight." He produced glazed donuts and poured two cups of coffee, handing one over to me.

I took a sip. "What did you put in the coffee?"

"Brandy—jus' enuff to take the edge off our nerves."

"Are you nervous, too?"

"Sure I am. I'm a mechanic, remember? I don' rob banks fer a livin'."

We sat in the darkness drinking brandy-laced coffee and eating donuts while watching the falling snow cover the windshield.

"McGerk, after you pay off that engine analyzer, what are you going to do with the rest of your half of the money?"

McGerk lit a cigarette, cracked open the truck window, and scratched his stubble, deep in thought.

"Well, all my life I been grubbin' around fixin' machines—cars, trucks, motorcycles, snowmobiles, outboards—anything with an engine. That's whut I always been good at. But I been thinkin', I'd like t'have a business where I could go t'work wearin' a clean shirt an' it'd stay clean all day. Mebbe get a nice place on the highway with gas pumps an' a garage fer repairs and lubes. But I'd get a couple of teenage grease monkeys workin' fer me t'do th'dirty work. I'd stay inside at the cash register takin' in th'money fer gas, repairs, an' food."

"You'd sell food?"

"Why not? Lots'a them gas stations sell all kinds'a stuff these days. People gas up an' pick up milk, bread, an' beer at the same time. Hell, I'd prob'ly even get one'a them damned PC's so's I could keep track of inventory an' figgur out my profits."

"My gawd, McGerk, I thought the only thing you ever wanted to do was repair cars."

"That's whut ya thought, huh? Well, I'm tired of bein' dirty all'a time. When I quit work at the end of the day I look in the mirror an' all I see is grease. No matter how hard I scrub I can't get it off. I can't go t'nice places an' meet classy women like th'one you got. Only chicks I stand a chance with are drinkin' bar whiskey an' beer down at the Wild Goose."

The subject of women instantly resurrected the painful memory of Chris's exit only hours before. I definitely planned to take her to Green Bay for a romantic weekend once I paid off the credit card with the bank's money.

"I thought you *liked* the Wild Goose," I said, trying to keep my mind off of Chris.

"I do. When yer a grubby bastard like me, without any money or class, that's the only kind'a place where y'feel at home. Worst thing is, after awhile ya get *used* to what'cha are an' don' even care.

"But I care *now*. I want sumthin' better. Hell, I never figgured on stealin' anything, but it's th'only way I kin see t'make it happen."

"Do you really think we'll get enough money to make things better for ourselves?"

"I sure as hell hope so. I ain't gonna do *this* again."

The brandy in the coffee was making me introspective and I kept talking. "You know, McGerk, it's ironic. When I first met you I thought you were just some grease-covered, ignorant lout living from one day to the next with no thought about the future. That first day in town, I couldn't wait to get out of that damned garage of yours because you made me so uncomfortable. It's crazy how things work out. If I don't get back together with Chris, you'll be the only friend I have."

Straightfaced, McGerk said, "Funny you should say that. When ya brought yer Olds in that day, I figgured you fer sum egghead dude from the big city with his head up his butt who didn't know jack about what he was getting into movin' up here. Now that I know ya a li'l better . . .," he paused, "I see I wuz right."

Now grinning, McGerk wiped a circle of condensation from his side of the truck window and stared out at the falling snow.

12

"Damn, y'look good in that outfit," McGerk joshed, trying to ease the tension. "You'll prob'ly wanna buy a flashy snowmobile wardrobe when ya get that new sled with yer share of th'money."

We'd just gathered up the GMC owner's clothing from the rear seat of the stolen truck and gotten dressed. I was decked out in wild purple padded pants and jacket with a wide black and white checked band running across the chest and under the armpits. "SKI-DOO"--in large white letters--ran up each pant leg. McGerk's garish outfit was similar.

"McGerk, I gotta pee."

"So pee, but use them rubber gloves so's ya don't leave any fingerprints on th'zipper. I dunno know if they kin take prints offa that or not."

By eight-thirty it was light enough to see, though the snow was still falling pretty good. The trucks, trailer, and snowmobiles were beneath a thick white blanket.

McGerk quickly got the two sleds hot-wired and running and drove them off the trailer. He topped off the fuel tanks from the gas can that he'd brought along and quickly made a minor tuning adjustment to one of the engines.

Satisfied, he pointed toward one of the sleds. "That one works pretty much like mine. You take it."

I got on the snowmobile and drove slowly around the meadow for fifteen minutes, getting the feel of the machine.

McGerk motioned me back to the trucks. He handed me one of the two empty duffel bags, and I tied it to the back of my sled.

"Ya got th'note?"

I unzipped the right pocket of the stolen jacket and showed him the envelope containing the holdup note.

"Need t'pee again?" he asked.

I shook my head.

"Okay, let's go. In this snow, I'm gonna take 'er slow. Stay in my tracks all th'way."

We headed off into the woods in tandem, more or less on the same path we'd taken weeks before.

Riding on the back of the MACH 1 during the dry run was one thing, but negotiating the same cross-country trek while piloting a strange snowmobile through heavily falling snow was something else. It required intense concentration—keeping my balance on the rough terrain, staying in McGerk's tracks, and dodging stray tree branches. McGerk glanced back from time to time, making sure I was still with him. The whole situation gave me a chilling sense of the unreal, and the strong scent of aftershave belonging to the owner of the stolen helmet provided an additional eerie touch.

All traces of our earlier dry run were covered by new snow, but McGerk expertly navigated his way through the area. After twenty minutes we arrived at the edge of the woods directly across the highway from the Hematite First National Bank.

We stopped but stayed within the cover of the trees. McGerk pulled up his helmet visor and glanced at his wristwatch. He pointed to the bank's empty parking lot at the front entrance.

"Good—no customers. See them cars in back of th'building? A

coupl'a tellers'll get in one a them in a few minutes an' go off on their coffee break. Then we move in."

He was right. At ten o'clock sharp, two women came out of the rear entrance of the bank, got in a car, and drove away.

"Let's go," McGerk said and gunned his snowmobile.

We crossed Highway 41—almost devoid of traffic in the snowstorm—and pulled into the bank parking lot. We'd no sooner stopped when a pickup truck pulled in, and a guy with a checkbook in his hand got out.

We sat on the idling snowmobiles, a scant twenty feet away, with our backs turned to the customer as he entered the front door.

McGerk cracked open his visor a slit and leaned over to me. "Stay cool. That's Arne Kinnunen—prob'ly just cashin' a check. He'll be out in a coupl'a minutes. We just wait."

Kinnunen came out, got into his pickup truck, and drove away.

McGerk handed me his duffel bag and punched me on the shoulder like a coach signaling a player to get into the game.

"Jus' remember, keep yer visor down, yer gloves on, an' yer mouth shut."

Carrying the two duffel bags, I entered the bank. My heart was pounding in my ears, and I was having trouble breathing inside the closed helmet.

Maria Grazzelli was an attractive, thirty-something brunette—five-five, a busty figure, and a pretty face. My racing, panic-stricken mind slowed momentarily and wondered why McGerk wasn't still going out with her.

"Well, you're certainly dressed for the weather this morning," she said cheerfully. "I guess you snowmobilers enjoy being out in weather like this. Personally, I'd like to take a little vacation and go to Florida for some beach time."

I handed her the note.

She put on a pair of reading glasses and squinted, holding the note at varying distances to bring the print into focus.

"These are my old-prescription glasses, so I can't see too well this morning," Maria confided. She laughed embarrassedly. "Would you believe I stepped on my good ones last night?"

McGerk and I had elected to make the note the same size as an ordinary bank-deposit slip. We didn't want to attract attention with a big piece of paper covered with large, scary, mismatched black words glued to it. Consequently, we'd used the *Mining Journal's* regular-text, ten-point print. It was all uniform and the instructions fit nicely on the slip, but it was small.

She frowned, turned the slip around, and pointed. "I'm sorry, what is this word?"

I almost spoke, but caught myself. I made a writing motion with my right hand.

She got the message and handed me one of the bank's tablets with their logo at the top.

"Lost your voice? I think you'd feel a lot better if you weren't out in weather like this."

I tried to grab the bank pen that dangled from a chain on the counter, but the thick snowmobile gloves were unwieldy and the pen kept slipping out of my grasp. Finally, I steadied the pen sufficiently to write:

ROBBERY

in big block letters on the pad. I turned the pad around and pushed it in front of her.

Maria Grazzelli looked at the word in disbelief. She stared into my visor, saw the ski mask, and became frightened. "Omigawd!"

With difficulty I grabbed the pen again and wrote:

KEEP YOUR VOICE DOWN

She looked at this message, glanced behind her at Arne Laxso's closed door, and nodded her head vigorously.

I placed the duffel bags on the counter, pushed them toward her, and jabbed my gloved finger at the hold-up note, indicating that she should make another stab at reading it.

Maria took the note, this time looking at it more intensely. She moved her lips as she attempted to decipher each word.

"I'm sorry, but I can't make out this . . ." She stopped in mid sentence, realized she was talking in a loud voice, and took the pad and wrote:

WHAT IS THE LONG WORD THAT BEGINS WITH A D?

She pushed the pad back to me.

I snatched at the bank's pen, and again it squirted out of my glove. I yanked the glove off in frustration, grabbed the pen in my bare hand and wrote:

DENOMINATIONS

Maria nodded quickly and finished reading the note, then wrote:

I DON'T UNDERSTAND ABOUT THE CART WITH THE CASHBOX.

As McGerk had predicted, the inner vault door was wide open and I had a direct view inside. There was no wheeled cart or metal cashbox in the vault. I wrote:

WHERE IS THE METAL CASHBOX?

Maria wrote:

WHAT METAL CASHBOX?

The thickly padded snowmobile gear was getting very warm. The ski mask was itching. Sweat poured down my ribs, and while McGerk claimed it couldn't happen, my helmet visor was beginning to fog up. I grabbed the pad and wrote:

EMPTY YOUR CASH DRAWER

Maria nodded and fumbled with her currency drawer, got it open, and began putting money into one of the duffel bags. When her drawer was empty, I motioned to her to go to the other teller stations and empty those drawers.

Maria took the pad. The top page was now full, so she ripped it off and started on the next page, scribbling:

THOSE DRAWERS ARE LOCKED. THE TELLERS WHO HAVE THE KEYS ARE OUT FOR COFFEE

I cursed to myself, snatched both duffel bags—one still completely empty—grabbed my right glove off the floor, and took the two sheets of paper containing Maria's and my messages. I dashed for the door but suddenly remembered that my fingerprints were on the pen. I ran back to the counter and yanked the pen loose, chain and all, and jammed it into my jacket pocket.

"We have some *free* pens you could have had," Maria called after me.

13

*I*n the months I'd known McGerk I'd never seen him even mildly upset, but he was really angry now. He stomped around the room, slammed a fist into the wall, and then delivered a vicious kick to the sofa where I was sitting.

He jabbed a finger at the stacks of sorted bills that were lying on the coffee table. "TWENNY-SIX HUNDRED THIRTY-TWO DOLLARS!" he yelled. "FER CRISSAKE, THAT WON' EVEN BUY A GOOD USED CAR!"

We had made stacks of ones, fives, tens, and twenties. There were only a few fifty- and hundred-dollar bills.

"She gave me everything in her drawer, and the other drawers were locked," I said. "There wasn't any metal cashbox in the vault."

"That box hadda be there somewheres. If ya'd looked around, ya would'a spotted it."

"Hey, mastermind," I shot back, "when was the last time you cased that bank—last *winter*? Things change! Maybe they get their armored-car deliveries on a different day now. Maybe their metal cashbox rusted out like all the damned cars around here."

"It wuz a dumb mistake t'take you on as a partner. I should'a done it myself."

"That's right. You'd be independently wealthy now with the whole twenty-six hundred and thirty-two dollars for yourself!"

The getaway had worked exactly as planned. We'd escaped into the woods on the snowmobiles, reached the meadow without incident, left all of the stolen equipment there, drove back to Ishpeming in McGerk's truck, and over to my apartment to count the loot.

In fact, the whole caper went flawlessly—except for one small thing. We'd gotten less than one and a half percent of the cash we'd expected.

"I gotta get over an' open up th'garage," McGerk muttered, calming down somewhat. "Don't wanna raise any suspicion by stayin' closed."

"Do you want your share?"

McGerk snorted sarcastically. "Hang onto it fer now, but don' spend any. We gotta take a closer look at them bills t'make sure none of 'em are marked. Be careful of them stacks of fives and tens with the paper strips still on 'em. Sometimes they're rigged with colored dye that gets on yer fingers when ya pull 'em apart."

"Do you trust me with all the money?" I was thinking about the harsh words we'd just exchanged.

McGerk headed for the door. "Sure I trust ya. Yer too dumb t'be a crook. Jus' find a safe place to stash it."

At 5 P.M. there was still one Michigan State Police unit at the Hematite First National Bank. Through the open door of the manager's office I could see Arne Laxso talking to a uniformed officer.

I'd hurried to the bank after spending an unproductive afternoon at the flooring mill. Not arriving at work until noon, I'd told the office manager that I had been sick to my stomach all morning. My gray complexion verified the story effectively.

As luck would have it, Maria Grazzelli was the next available teller. "Yes, may I help you?"

"I'd like to rent a safe-deposit box."

She handed me a form to fill out. "I guess you heard that we had quite a bit of excitement here this morning."

"Oh?"

"You didn't hear? The bank was robbed."

"You're kidding! What happened?"

By now, Maria had the story well rehearsed. "They came up on snowmobiles—two of them. One stayed outside as a lookout and the other one—the leader—came in and demanded money."

She leaned forward and paused for dramatic effect. "I was the only teller in the bank when it happened."

"My gawd—is that right? That must have been a frightening experience."

"Let me tell you. He gave me a note demanding that I fill up his two bags with money. I think he had one of those automatic weapons."

"An automatic weapon?" I exclaimed. "Did you see it?"

"Well, not really. But the outline of it underneath his jacket was hard to miss. No question he meant business."

"Did they get much money?"

Maria pursed her lips. "Well, the bank directors have ordered an audit, and I can't talk about the amount of money taken. The local television people were here, so you might hear more about it on the six o'clock news."

I completed the form and slid it back to her. Maria picked up a set of keys and opened a gate, allowing me to follow her into the vault.

"Were you able to get a good look at the robber?" I asked while Maria scanned the array of safe-deposit boxes.

"He was wearing one of those snowmobile helmets with a ski mask underneath." She turned and stared at me. "But I'll never forget those eyes—cold and hard. I tell you, the man was a natural-born killer. If I ever see him again—mask or no mask—I'll know him by those eyes."

I gave her the warmest smile I could muster. "You were lucky to escape with your life."

Maria nodded emphatically. She located the proper box, inserted both keys, opened the door, and removed the inner metal container, handing it to me along with my key.

"You can use the little cubicle outside of the vault. Let me know when you're finished."

"Thank you."

In the privacy of the cubicle I removed two packets from the inside pocket of my coat. Each one, wrapped in brown paper and securely sealed with mailing tape, measured about three inches wide by six inches long. I slipped them into the metal container and closed the cover.

"Okay, I'm all done," I called out to Maria.

She came back and locked the box using both of our keys.

"Thank you for doing business with Hematite First National Bank," Maria said cheerfully as I left.

McGerk showed up at my place just before six. I told him what I'd done.

"Ya brought th'money back t'the *bank*?"

"Why not? It's the last place anybody would think to look for it."

"Ya gotta weird sense a humor," McGerk muttered.

We opened a couple of beers and turned on the TV, eager to hear the local six o'clock news.

As expected, the robbery was the lead story. A field reporter standing in the blowing snow in front of the Hematite First National Bank building described the robber's entrance into the bank, the robbery note, and the getaway into the woods on the stolen snowmobiles.

She completed her segment, saying, "The bank is currently performing an audit and hasn't released the amount of money taken, but apparently the robbers didn't score as much as they could have under more favorable conditions. They had bad luck with the weather. The regular Friday-morning cash delivery by armored car had been delayed due to bad highway conditions south of here."

"We'll wait fer a snowstorm," I said sarcastically, mimicking McGerk's U.P. accent.

"Shaddup."

The reporter continued. "State police, assisted by local Hiawatha Snowmobile Club members, followed the route taken by the robbers through the woods. They discovered two snowmobiles and a GMC pickup truck with an attached snowmobile trailer in a clearing a few miles south of the bank. The equipment had been stolen from the Woodlands Motel parking lot on US-41 sometime between early evening and the time of the robbery."

"Won' find it till th'spring thaw," I said, mimicking him again.

"I'm warnin' ya," McGerk snapped.

The next segment was an interview with an Ishpeming Police detective who stated that the investigation was being hampered by the bad weather and that they had no further information at this time.

Maria Grazzelli appeared next with a detailed account of the robber's menacing demeanor. She didn't mention anything about a gun, however. The automatic weapon was apparently an embellishment reserved exclusively for her afternoon bank customers.

With a voice-over from the TV anchorman, they displayed the

holdup note I'd composed. The focus was perfect, every word clearly legible.

The final segment was a partial film clip from the bank's security camera showing me gaily clad in the stolen electric purple helmet, jacket, and pants. I moved jerkily up to the counter, ripped out the pen and chain, and fled out the front door.

"Ever think ya'd be a TV star?" McGerk asked.

14

A half-hour later McGerk and I were sitting down to TV dinners when there was a savage pounding on my front door.

We looked at each other in panic.

"Is there a back way outta here?" McGerk whispered.

"The patio door. But your truck's parked out front. If it's the cops, they already know you're here."

With dread I got up and opened the door.

Chris brushed past me into the living room.

"*You* did it," she said tonelessly. "The two of you."

"Did what?"

"Robbed that bank this morning."

I tried to scoff. "What are you talking about?"

"The holdup note they showed on the news. I almost jumped out of my skin when I saw it. You wrote it. I'm your writing teacher, remember? Every phrase was your style.

"And when they showed the shot from the surveillance camera, I knew for sure. I didn't have to see your face. I could tell by the walk."

McGerk said, "Him? A bank robber? He's too stupid t'be a bank robber."

Chris turned on him. "That's true. Then, *you* must have been the brains of this two-man mob."

Simmering, she turned back to me, "It all fits—almost killing yourself snowmobiling. You had to learn how to drive one for the getaway. And then late last night, coming up with that story about the power outage at the flooring mill. Your idiot friend here called and gave you the last-minute go-ahead on the job, and you needed enough time to steal the snowmobiles."

My legs began to buckle. I carefully guided my body over to the sofa and proceeded to confess everything.

When I was finished, McGerk snapped, "I'm sure as hell glad that Chris wuz the first one t'lean on you instead of th'cops."

That seemed to make Chris even more angry. "What makes you think *I* won't turn the two of you in? Him I can understand," she said, pointing at McGerk, "but *you*? You're an educated man. What on earth made you do such an incredibly stupid thing?"

"Didn' even get that much," McGerk mumbled. "Twenny-six hundred an' thir. . ."

"SHUT UP!" Chris shouted. "I'm not talking to you!"

"I never would have done it, except for you," I said miserably.

"For me? What moldy old movie did you get *that* line from?"

"Chris, it's true. Everything I told you about being a high-paid software consultant at the mill was a lie. I got laid off from my job in California and soon ran out of money, so I decided to try my hand at writing the book I've been thinking about for so long. I moved up here to write it.

"Then I met you. It might have been love at first sight, I don't know. But I couldn't tell you the truth. I was afraid you'd think I was just another low-life bum like your ex and dump me. I started charging everything on my credit card—even this apartment—and before I knew it I was in way over my head. I tried to think of a way to pay off that credit card but couldn't come up with one. The robbery was the last resort."

Chris stood there for a long moment. Finally, she produced a handkerchief and dabbed at the tears rolling down her cheeks. Then, very softly said, "I thought you were running around with another woman."

I jumped up from the sofa and grabbed her by the shoulders. "I'd *never* do that! I *love* you. If I didn't, I wouldn't be in this damned fix now."

McGerk edged toward the door, putting on his mackinaw. "This's gettin' a li'l personal. I'll be goin'."

"SIT DOWN!" Chris yelled again. "I'm not through with you yet!"

McGerk stood indecisively for a second, then went into the kitchen and opened up a can of beer. He grabbed the bottle of brandy out of the cupboard, took a big mouthful of beer, and topped the can off with brandy. Then he put a grimy thumb over the hole in the top of the beer can and shook it up.

"Where's the money?" Chris asked.

"It's in the bank," I said.

"Don't get smart. I mean the money you took during the robbery."

"That's th'money he means," McGerk said. "He put it back in th'bank."

"I was really nervous having it here, so I wrapped it up, brought it to the bank, and put it in a safe-deposit box."

Chris gave me an odd look. "The *same* bank?"

"Yes."

She closed her eyes, took off her glasses, and rubbed the bridge of her nose. "Why is it that I keep getting mixed up with weird guys?"

She went into the kitchen and poured two inches of brandy into a water glass. It looked like a good idea, so I did the same. We all sat down at the dining-room table and drank in silence for several minutes.

Chris finally spoke up. "First thing in the morning, turn yourselves in to the Ishpeming police and tell them where the money is."

McGerk and I stared at her for a long moment.

"Y'gonna turn us in if we don't?" McGerk asked.

"I'd be an accessory after the fact if I didn't. That's also a crime."

"You'd send me to prison?" I asked quietly.

Chris tried to take a sip of brandy but instead broke down sobbing. "I don't want to. I love you, don't you understand that? But we'd never make it with something like this hanging over our heads. If we're ever to have a chance together, we'll have to start with a clean slate—nothing to hide.

"You're both first-time offenders. If you turn yourselves in, that would be the first step toward rehabilitation and would bode well in your favor. With time off for good behavior, you'd probably only have to serve about five years. And I'll be there when you get out."

Chris stood up, dried her eyes, and put her coat on. "I'm leaving now, but please, please think about what I've said. Do it soon, before they somehow connect you with the robbery and take you in.

"But if you don't surrender to the police, I'll have no choice but to turn you in myself." She buttoned her coat and left.

McGerk said to me, "And yer in *love* with that woman?"

"'Turn yourselves in,'" he mimicked in a high-pitched voice. "Jezzuz, trust a woman to come up with that one. 'I'll be there when you get out,' she says. Who's gonna be there when *I* get out?"

He marched into the kitchen, popped open another beer, sipped, and poured a generous slug of brandy into the can.

"What does that taste like?" I asked.

"Try one. They call it a depth charge."

We sat on the sofa drinking depth charges, contemplating our situation.

"She's probably right," I said.

"Easy fer *you* t'say. She's givin' ya a—whaddaya call

it—ultimatum. Go th'straight an' narrow or that's it fer the luvvin'. Can you see anything in that deal fer *me*?"

"No, but think about it. We only got twenty-six hundred out of it. That doesn't even put a dent in our money problems. But if they catch us, it'll be as bad as if we took a million dollars. Chris's right. We can probably get a better deal if we return the money and face the music."

"You ever been in jail?" McGerk asked.

"Of course not."

"I wuz—years ago. Drunk an' disorderly. Ishpeming lockup fer a day an' a half. Felt like six months. Ya don' even wanna *think* 'bout doin' five years."

We drank another depth charge.

"We could mail the money back to the bank with an anonymous letter," I suggested.

"Some bank secretary openin' th'mail could pocket the cash. We'd be out th'money, an' th'cops'd *still* be lookin' fer us."

"Mail it to the police?"

"Same problem—some clerk at th'police department could get tempted . . . it's *cash* fer crissakes."

We drank another depth charge.

"There's another way," I said finally.

"What's that?"

"We pull the robbery in reverse."

McGerk lit a cigarette, scratched his stubble, and looked into his beer can. "Maybe this stuff is gettin' t'me 'cause I think I missed that. Run it by me again."

15

*E*arly the next morning I called Chris. "McGerk and I have come up with a slightly different plan."

"I'm going to hang up. I don't want to hear this."

"No, wait—it's good. We give the money back and apologize."

"There's more, I can tell," Chris said.

I told her about the reverse robbery.

"That's got to be the most idiotic thing I've ever heard."

"No, it's not. It's a way to repent without going to prison. I get the money out of the safe-deposit box. McGerk steals another snowmobile—we only need one now. We take the money back to the bank with a note saying that we're sorry we took it, put the note right up to the surveillance camera to get it on record, then give it to the teller along with the money. Jump on the sled and make our getaway.

"It'll make all the papers—the bank robbers who turned over a new leaf and brought the money back to the bank. Public opinion will be on our side. The police are busy enough dealing with real criminals without trying to crack a case where the robbers have brought the loot back. I'll bet you that within a week all the cops on the case will be reassigned. Case closed."

"What do you guys drink when you cook up these schemes?"

"We have to wait until Monday when the bank opens so I can get the money out of the safe-deposit box, but it's going to work, I promise you."

"Then they'll only be hunting you down for stealing snowmobiles."

This time McGerk had a simpler plan for stealing a sled. On Sunday night we were sitting in the cocktail lounge of the Chippewa Lodge, a motel, bar, and restaurant on Highway 41, west of Ishpeming. The place was filled with thirsty snowmobilers fresh off the trails.

McGerk casually sipped his beer and gazed across the crowded bar. "See that heavy-set guy an' th'blonde woman with the bleach job?" he muttered in a low voice. "Th'ones who just ordered another beer."

"Yes."

"They own that Yamaha touring sled parked a li'l ways down the road, away from th'parking-lot lights. That's th'one we're gonna take."

"How do you know they're the owners?"

"Their pants. Got YAMAHA down th'legs in big white letters. That sled's the only Yamaha out there. Downstate snowmobilers always buy clothes t'match their sleds. If they ain't stayin' at the lodge fer the night, they'll at least be workin' on them fresh beers fer awhile."

McGerk leaned over closer. "Let's go. Jus' follow me out th'door."

We threw some money on the bar and headed for the door. McGerk, hardly slowing down, grabbed the two Yahama helmets and jackets from the wall pegs filled with snowmobile clothing. He handed me a jacket and helmet.

Outside he gave me the keys to his truck. "You drive about a mile back towards Ishpeming. Park on the shoulder an' wait. I'll be along in a few minutes."

I did as he instructed. Five minutes later McGerk roared up on the

Yahama snowmobile. He quickly ran it up onto the trailer and covered it with the MACH 1's tarp. We sped off into the night.

Monday morning I called in sick again, went to the bank as soon as they opened, and retrieved the money from the safe-deposit box. Before leaving I glanced around. It only took a few seconds to locate the bank's surveillance camera since the TV news clip had revealed the camera's angle.

I hurried over to McGerk's place where he was waiting outside. He opened the garage door, backed his truck inside, and hooked up the trailer holding the tarp-covered Yamaha. We took off immediately, pressed for time since we'd decided that ten o'clock was still the safest hour to enter the bank, with most of the tellers away on their coffee break.

This time McGerk simply pulled the pickup and trailer onto a small side road close to one of the groomed trails that ran past the bank. We stopped and quickly ran the Yamaha off the trailer, hopped on, and followed the trail for about a half-mile.

At ten o'clock we emerged from the woods, again directly across from the bank. Most of the tellers were gone on their coffee break, and there weren't any customer's cars in the parking lot. I hopped off the stolen sled and went into the bank, not nearly so nervous this time.

Maria Grazzelli began to smile but then registered alarm when she spotted the ski mask under my helmet. Her fear was combined with bewilderment as I reached up and held the new paste-up note in front of the surveillance camera. That done, I walked up and slapped the note down in front of her. This time I'd used much larger letters so both Maria and the camera could clearly pick up the text.

Maria shot a glance at the big, ugly words on the note but didn't read it. "Omigawd—two robberies in less than a week—omigawd." She began pulling money out of her cash drawer.

I grabbed one of the bank's note pads, scribbled a message, and shoved it back to her.

THIS ISN'T A ROBBERY. READ THE DAMNED NOTE.

Maria read my message and looked up, confused. I jabbed a gloved finger at the paste-up note I'd brought in. With effort she read it, her lips mouthing each word.

REMAIN CALM AND KEEP YOUR VOICE DOWN. THIS IS NOT A ROBBERY. THE PACKAGE I'M GOING TO GIVE YOU CONTAINS THE STOLEN MONEY IN ITS ENTIRETY—$2632—THE EXACT AMOUNT TAKEN LAST WEEK.

MY PARTNER AND I APOLOGIZE FOR ANY INCONVENIENCE WE MAY HAVE CAUSED THE BANK. WE ARE TRULY SORRY AND HAVE NO INTENTION OF COMMITTING ANY FURTHER CRIMES.

HOWEVER, WE ARE STILL ARMED AND DANGEROUS, SO DO NOT CONSIDER ACTIVATING THE ALARM.

McGerk had insisted on the last sentence, concerned that the tone of the rest of the note made us sound like such pussycats that Maria might get brave and take matters into her own hands.

Remembering the drill from the past Friday, Maria took the scratch pad and wrote:

YOU'RE REALLY BRINGING THE MONEY BACK?

Last night McGerk and I had carefully wiped off each of the stolen bills to eliminate the possibility of fingerprints and placed them in a plastic Baggie. I took the Baggie from my pocket and pushed it toward her.

Maria continued writing:

THERE'S ONE PROBLEM.

I wrote:

WHAT?

She wrote:

BANK DOESN'T KNOW HOW MUCH MONEY WAS STOLEN.

I stared at the pad with disbelief, then wrote:

WHAT DO YOU MEAN?

Maria wrote:

THE BANK INSTALLED NEW COMPUTER SYSTEM LAST THURSDAY. COMPUTER SPECIALIST STILL CHECKING IT OUT. UNTIL HE'S FINISHED, BANK WON'T KNOW HOW MUCH WAS STOLEN.

I was really pissed now and wrote:

I'M ONE OF THE ROBBERS, AND I'M TELLING YOU, $2632 IS WHAT WAS STOLEN

Someone behind me said, "Is this transaction gonna take much longer? I'm on my coffee break and have to get back to work."

I whipped my head around to face a large burly man standing in line behind me. He'd walked in without me noticing.

Panicking, I plunged my left hand into my jacket pocket and made a jabbing gesture toward him, indicating I had a hidden gun and was ready to use it.

Seeing that, Maria fell to the floor in a dead faint.

I grabbed the paste-up note, the scratch pad, and the Baggie of money and ran out of the bank.

16

"I DON' GAWDAMN *BELIEVE* IT!"

McGerk was raging mad again, but this time he was behind the wheel of the pickup and driving like a lunatic down a narrow, winding county road. We were speeding back to Ishpeming after dumping the stolen sled, helmets, and jackets. The old truck skidded dangerously at every curve, but McGerk somehow straightened it out each time.

I looked out the rear window to see if anyone was following us. "What was I supposed to do? Leave the money there when the bank hasn't even figured out how much is missing?"

"Y'mean t'tell me that th'bank ain't gonna know whut we took till the computer tells 'em? Don' people know how to count money anymore?"

"Nowadays computers run everything. When a new system gets installed, it'll have software bugs. It may take a week or more to get it working right."

McGerk scowled through the windshield at the road ahead. "T'hell with it. We keep th'money an' hope fer th'best."

"What about Chris? She might have something to say about that."

McGerk shot me a wary look, obviously worried about what Chris might do. "Hell, it'll be all over the news tonight. Everybody'll see th'note ya jammed in front of th'security camera. She'll at least know we *tried* t'take th'money back."

McGerk dropped me off at my apartment. I emptied a large box of Grape-Nuts onto a newspaper, stuffed the stolen money into the bottom of the box, and poured enough cereal back to fill it up. The box went up on the top shelf in my kitchen cupboard. I quickly changed clothes and hurried off to work.

"What's the matter? You got morning sickness?" the office manager asked. "How far along are you?" He chuckled at his own wit, and the secretary giggled.

I mumbled some lame excuse about an upset stomach—true enough—and trudged off to my work station.

I tried to reach Chris from the pay phone in the corridor all afternoon, but she had a heavy Monday schedule at the university. I didn't leave a message. Telling her answering machine what really happened was too risky.

Just before quitting time, Uncle Paul knocked on my cubicle door frame as I was halfheartedly entering columns of lumber data into the PC.

"Edna's makin' yer favorite tonight—meatballs. Knew you'd wanna come over fer supper." More of a command than an invitation.

I smiled and told him I'd be there. I wasn't exactly in the mood for socializing with Paul and Edna, but if I stayed at home, McGerk would come over to watch the six o'clock news and want to rehash and bitch about today's botched bank job. I wasn't up to that.

After a humongous meal of meatballs, gravy, mashed potatoes, and buttered string beans, Paul and I retired to the living room to watch the six o'clock news. Edna served coffee and freshly baked Finnish coffee bread for dessert. I reluctantly accepted a piece of the buttered coffee bread although I had no appetite for it. The meatballs were still sitting in my stomach like lumps of lead. Robbing banks wasn't compatible with good digestion.

The action at the Hematite Bank was the lead story on the six o'clock news. I sat back, trying to appear only mildly interested.

For the second time in three days, a sober-faced reporter stood in front of the Hematite First National Bank. Behind her, the parking lot was filled with police cars.

"The snowmobile bank robbers have struck again, and once more the Hematite First National Bank was the target. The M.O. was the same as last Friday's robbery with one of the robbers, dressed in snowmobile gear, entering the bank and giving the teller a note. This time, however, the robbery was foiled by a bank customer. Without getting any money, the robber fled to the parking lot where his accomplice was waiting on a snowmobile, and again they escaped into the woods."

"What is this town coming to?" Edna exclaimed. "Two bank robberies in less than a week."

"Never had much use fer them snowmobilers," Paul said sourly. "Buzzin' around all hours of th'night on them damned noisy machines. Betcha these guys're from Detroit or Chicago or somewhere down there where all them crooks live."

The TV reporter continued. "Maria Grazzelli, the teller who was forced to turn the money over during Friday's robbery, was once again the only teller in the bank. She was so overcome by this second robbery attempt that she fell to the floor unconscious.

"When the robber entered the bank today, for some unknown

reason he reached up and placed the note in front of the surveillance camera. As you will see, the note is partially obscured but it clearly signaled the robber's intent."

The next film clip was taken from the bank's surveillance camera. Looking Darth Vaderlike in the helmet, I was thrusting the paste-up note to the camera lens. But in my haste, I had clutched the note in mid-page with the bulky glove. The resulting paper wrinkles made it impossible to read much of the text, but what *was* legible were several words on the top and bottom of the note:

CALM AND KEEP YOUR VOICE DOWN
A ROBBERY.

ARMED AND DANGEROUS
DO NOT CONSIDER ACTIVATING THE ALARM.

I stared at the TV in disbelief as the reporter continued, "During an interview at the bank, Ms. Grazzelli was asked to review the surveillance-camera film to give the police additional information about the full text of the note, which she had seen during the robbery attempt. Dazed and confused from the ordeal, Ms. Grazzelli admitted that she wasn't sure what had been written on the note that the robber took with him."

The coffee bread slipped out of my hand and fell to the carpet, buttered side down.

"You all right, Joe?" Paul asked.

Edna picked up the coffee bread and attempted to rub the butter off the carpet. "Look at him, Paul. The robbery is upsetting him. Joe moved from Los Angeles to get away from that sort of thing, and now he sees it happening right here in Ishpeming. Drink some of your coffee, Joe, you'll feel better."

The field reporter was now interviewing the man who had come up behind me in the bank. His name was Bruno LaFarge.

"Mr. LaFarge, you're a real hero today. What were you thinking when the bank robber turned and faced you?"

Thoroughly enjoying his fifteen minutes of fame, LaFarge's broad face split into a self-assured grin. "Guy was a hard case alright—you could tell by those eyes behind that mask. When I confronted him, he went for a gun in his jacket pocket, but I stared him down. That's when he ran for the door."

"Bank officials say that you saved the Hematite First National a lot of money," the reporter said. "There was over a hundred and fifty thousand dollars in the open vault."

Coffee slopped all over my pants.

The news anchorman presented the final robbery segment. "Arne Laxso, the bank manager, informed authorities this afternoon that the bank has completed its audit, revealing that the take from Friday's robbery was over forty-two thousand dollars."

"*Forty-two thousand dollars?*" I gasped.

Edna grew concerned. "Paul, turn off the TV. Joe's sensitive, just like his mother."

Grudgingly, Paul picked up the remote, but I raised my hand. "No, leave it on."

The anchorman concluded with, "These two men are considered armed and very dangerous. If anyone has any information pertaining to their whereabouts, please contact the Michigan State Police."

I blinked my eyes at the TV screen, stunned. For once, Paul was sympathetic.

"Don't let this stuff get to ya, Joe. Hell, forty-two thousand ain't much fer a bank robbery these days."

The phone was ringing when I opened the apartment door. I grabbed the receiver.

Chris's voice shook with anger. "I thought you loved me and knew that I love *you*. But no, that wasn't enough. You had to try for the big score. Well, let me tell you something mister; I won't ruin my life being an accessory after the fact. You leave me no choice but to go to the police."

I gestured wildly in the air. "No, don't—don't do that. What you saw on the news is all wrong—a mistake. Come over here right now and I'll straighten it out. I mean it—come over here NOW!"

I'd no sooner hung up the phone when it rang again.

"Y'owe me twenny-one thousand dollars," McGerk snarled. "How did'ja manage it? Ya must'a dumped forty grand in th'snow somewheres after we left th'bank an' then picked it up later. I should'a known better. I knew ya wuz a weasel th'first day I laid eyes on ya."

"Shut up. There *is* no forty grand. Get your ass over here right away. Chris is on her way and we're going to straighten this out."

17

*M*cGerk angrily brushed past me at the door, then abruptly wheeled around in my living room to face me. "Okay, start talkin'."

I took the offensive. "Do you actually think I took forty-two thousand out of that bank and managed to hide forty of it somewhere out in the woods? In a snowstorm? Hell, I don't know where I am in the woods in *good* weather. I'd *never* be able to find the money again. And if I'd hidden it in that sled or the stolen truck, the cops would have found it by now. They probably went over that stuff with a fine-tooth comb."

I'd no sooner gotten McGerk calmed down when Chris arrived. "This'd better be good," she stormed.

I took the holdup note and the scratch-pad correspondence between Maria Grazzelli and me and put all of it in front of Chris.

After reading, she said, "My gawd, you really *were* trying to take the money back, weren't you?"

"Yes."

"It should'a worked, too." McGerk said angrily. "It don' take no rocket scientist t'hold a piece of paper up straight so's a dumb camera kin read it."

"You idiot, think about what you just said," I shot back. "It wouldn't have made any difference what happened in there today. The bank claims that over forty-two thousand is missing, and we were trying to return a measly twenty-six hundred."

Chris reread the paste-up note, now thoroughly puzzled. "How could the bank come up with forty-two thousand missing?"

"I'm not sure. It could be a mistake in the new software system, but I doubt it. Those are sealed packages, thoroughly validated. Or someone could've goofed while entering data into the audit process, but that's also unlikely with all the checks and balances they have in the system. Or—and this is where I'm placing my bet—someone's dipping into the bank's money, besides us."

"Whaddaya mean?" McGerk asked.

"Embezzlement. With almost no one around, the robbery presented the perfect opportunity for someone left inside the bank to dip into the till. And I've got a hunch who it might be."

Chris looked surprised. "The teller?"

"Ms. Maria Grazzelli herself," I said.

McGerk looked absolutely astounded. "Maria?"

"It makes sense," Chris said. "She told the police that she was too upset to remember what your note said. Yet, those messages she wrote on the pad while you were standing there look to me like she was pretty clear-headed."

"Exactly," I replied. "She was frightened but not scared out of her wits. And how could she possibly forget a note stating that the robbers were bringing the money *back* to the bank?

"And I remember that when I went to put the money into a safe-deposit box, Maria was talking nonstop—telling me the whole story—until I asked her how much money had been taken. Then she clammed up."

"There had to be more money around than just what the tellers had in the cash drawers," Chris added thoughtfully. "What if someone comes in and wants to cash in five or ten thousand dollars worth of savings bonds? That's not unusual."

McGerk said, "Ya really think that after th'robbery on Friday morning Maria helped herself to cash from th'vault before she pushed th'alarm?"

"That's right," I replied. "With no one else in the bank, except Arne Laxso who was in the back office, she probably had several minutes before the other tellers got back from their coffee break. She could have hurried into the vault, taken forty thousand in packaged bills, put them into a big tote bag or something and taken it out and hidden it in her car before she pressed the alarm.

"And she's much sharper than we gave her credit for," I added. "Today when the police showed her the surveillance tape and she saw that most of the note couldn't be read, she just played it dumb—too distraught to remember any of the details, she claimed. Everyone thinks we got forty-two thousand and returned to the bank today to get more."

"The perfect frame-up," Chris said.

McGerk was finding it hard to believe that Maria would be capable of committing such an act. "But mebbe somebody else workin' in th'bank could'a lifted th'cash *before* th'robbery."

I shook my head. "Think about this. Suppose she's innocent, and someone else in the bank has helped themselves to the money. Maria is the only one who knows first-hand just how little money we really got, so when the bank completed the audit and declared forty-two thousand missing, Maria would have realized that something funny was going on since she couldn't possibly have had that much in her cash drawer. If she wasn't guilty of embezzlement she would have spoken up. But obviously, she hasn't said a word."

"I think I need a drink," McGerk muttered.

It was an excellent idea. Chris got the bottle and we all sat on the sofa and began downing straight brandy.

"Do you know this Grazzelli woman?" Chris asked McGerk.

I laughed. "He used to take her out. That's why I was the inside man at the bank. McGerk was afraid she'd recognize his eyeballs, even inside the helmet and mask."

Chris whipped off her glasses and looked at McGerk. "Is that why you looked so shaken when we mentioned Maria as a suspect? You used to go out with her?"

McGerk nodded.

"When was this?"

"Years back."

Chris pressed on. "Well, c'mon, tell us. Do you think she's capable of stealing that money?"

McGerk, suddenly moody, sighed and sipped his brandy, staring at the rug. "I dunno, purty hard t'believe. I jus' don' know."

"Tell us about you two," I said.

McGerk shrugged. "Ain't much t'tell. Wuz in th'bank one day an' asked her out. 'Okay,' she sez. Took her out mebbe a dozen times. Had a lotta fun at first, although she never would go to th'places I hang around in. Tried t'take her into the Wild Goose one night, but she wouldn't go in. Figured she wuz too good fer that, I guess. That's about it."

"Has she ever been married?" Chris asked.

"Nope."

"How old is she?" I asked McGerk.

McGerk thought a second. "Thirty-six."

"Well, the Hematite First National Bank just presented her with a dowry," Chris said.

"That's nice for her, but we're screwed," I added. "The cops are after us, and if we're caught, we can't give the money back even though we want to. And if we try to blow the whistle on Maria, they'll just laugh at us."

McGerk took the brandy bottle and refilled everyone's glass.

Chris stared off into space. "You know, let's just suppose that you guys had all that money—all forty-two thousand. It still might not be too late to take it back to the bank with that wild reverse-robbery scheme of yours."

That surprised me. "You said yourself that it was the most idiotic thing you'd ever heard."

"You've convinced me that it's the only way to make certain that the money gets back safely, especially knowing what we do now about Maria Grazzelli. Besides, you two are getting pretty good at making snowmobile getaways."

I smiled at her. "You're shifting from an accessory after the fact to being an accomplice."

Chris nodded. "You're right. It must be the cheap booze that you serve here. I'm becoming a member of the mob.

"But back to the problem at hand—Maria deprived you of the chance to pull yourself out of this mess. We've got to get that money away from her."

She paused to organize her thoughts. "Now, listen to this. It's only been a few days since she took the cash. She knows the police will be keeping a close eye on everyone for awhile after the robbery—standard procedure. It'd be too risky for her to try to deposit the entire forty thousand in one account. Over time, she might make a number of smaller deposits in several banks or put it into safe-deposit boxes. But I'll bet she hasn't had a chance to do anything with the money yet, because remember, this wasn't something she had planned in advance. Chances are she still has the entire forty thousand, and I'd guess it's stashed somewhere in her home."

"That would be a stupid place to keep it," I said.

"What else can she do? She can't trust anyone with it."

"So we toss her place while she's at work," McGerk offered.

"Too risky in broad daylight," Chris said. "The neighbors might spot you going in and out. Much better if it could be done at night when she's away."

I said, "But we don't know when, where, or even if she goes out at night or for that matter when she comes home."

Chris smiled craftily at me. "But we would if one of you took her out on a date."

"Maria Grazzelli? Are you serious?"

"Absolutely."

"She's four years older than I am," I said defensively.

Chris gasped in surprise. "We're trying to keep you out of jail, and you're worried about taking out an older woman?"

"McGerk took her out. Let him do it."

"She wouldn't go out with me," McGerk stated.

"Why not?"

"We went to a nice restaurant in Marquette one night. Maria liked t'go out t'dinner in Marquette—the better places. Couldn't afford 'em, but I usually went along with it. Anyway, we were havin' sumthin' expensive an' she looks down at my hands an' sez, 'Why can't you wash yer hands before ya pick me up?' Hell, I'd scrubbed till my hands were raw, but that car grease don' come off. I got mad as hell, an' we started yellin' at each other. First thing ya know the manager's askin' us t'leave. That wuz th'last time we went out. She wanted somebody with a li'l more class, I guess."

Chris listened to McGerk's story then turned to me. "Okay, it's up to you. While you're wining and dining Maria, McGerk goes over to her place and searches for the money. Can you jimmy a door lock, McGerk?"

McGerk grinned, relieved of the responsibility of entertaining Maria. "I kin jimmy *any* kind'a lock."

"Wait a minute," I said. "If McGerk finds the money, Maria will see that it's gone and figure that I was in on it, drawing her away from the house."

"So what?" Chris replied. "Who can she tell? In fact, she'd better hope that you two don't get caught after you bring the money back on the reverse robbery. You might tell the police where you got it from."

"What makes you so sure she'll go out with me?"

"Ask her if she wants to go to dinner at the Landmark Inn," Chris said. "That's how you hooked me."

18

*B*efore going to work the next morning, I drove over to the bank. I ignored the other tellers and got in line behind three women at Maria Grazzelli's window.

Having been confronted by an alleged armed bank robber on two successive workdays, Maria had become an overnight celebrity. Everyone was keen on hearing the gripping details, including, of course, the women in line ahead of me. I waited patiently while Maria provided a blow-by-blow account for each one of them.

I finally got to her window and promptly flashed my brightest smile. "My, aren't you the popular one."

"I guess you heard what happened, huh?" Maria said in a half-whisper, leaning forward in anticipation of launching into her story once again.

I appeared sympathetic and interested. "I saw it on the news last night. What a terrible thing to have happen to you twice."

"You know it. I actually fainted when he reached for his gun to shoot Mr. LaFarge. I fell over backwards and hit the floor like a brick. Here, look at this." She turned around and parted her thick black hair back to reveal an ugly purple lump on the back of her head.

For the next several minutes Maria proceeded to relate the details of my visit to the bank the previous day. Much of it didn't resemble the truth, as I knew it.

Pausing for breath she said, "Well, I'll stop wasting your time. What can I do for you today?"

I laughed lightheartedly. "You're not wasting my time. You have such an exciting way of telling a story that it sends shivers up my spine. However, I do have to get into my safe-deposit box again, if it's not too much trouble."

Smiling, Maria handed me the signature card. "No trouble at all." She verified my signature and grabbed her ring of keys. I followed her back into the vault.

I did a quick appraisal of Maria from behind. She was a little on the hefty side, but it fit her Mediterranean features. All in all, an attractive woman.

Maria inserted her key into the safe-deposit box lock. I quickly put my key in the lock before she could withdraw her hand, taking care to let my fingers slowly brush against the back of her wrist. She flashed me a quizzical look. I responded with my best lingering smile.

I removed the box and went into the privacy cubicle and closed the door. This time, however, there was no business to conduct since I'd left the cash back at the apartment in the bottom of the Grape-Nuts box. I was in the bank for an entirely different reason. I waited a few minutes before opening the cubicle door.

"I'm ready, Maria,"—the first time I'd used her name.

She slid off the teller's stool and walked toward me. I thought I detected a trace of a swivel in her hips.

I replaced the safe-deposit box, and Maria and I inserted our keys in the lock simultaneously. This time she left her hand on her key ring, waiting to see what I would do next. I covered her hand with mine, giving it a gentle squeeze.

"I know you may think this is crazy, me a bank customer and us being in the vault like this, but I've been thinking about you ever since

I was in here the other day. I don't believe in wasting time. Would you have dinner with me?"

For once, Maria was quiet, thinking. Finally she said, "When?"

"How about this evening at the Landmark Inn?"

She stared at me directly with dancing dark-brown eyes and a hint of a brazen smile. "You like to move fast, don't you?"

Chris and McGerk were at my apartment for a countdown strategy meeting before I left to pick up Maria at seven.

Chris had a small bag—a woman's beauty kit. She bent over my face, inspecting my nose.

"Hold still, you have a couple of long hairs growing out of one of your nostrils." She inserted the blades of a pair of manicure scissors and snipped.

"Oh, for crissakes, this is overkill," I complained.

"No, it's not. All women appreciate a well-groomed man."

McGerk leaned in closely behind Chris. "His eyebrows're lookin' a li'l shaggy, too."

"Shut up, McGerk," I said.

"We'll leave the eyebrows alone," Chris said. "Shaggy eyebrows give him an intellectual look."

She reached for a different pair of scissors and began trimming my sideburns.

I asked Chris, "Do you have any idea what it cost for two dinners at the Landmark that night we were there in December?"

Chris stopped cutting my hair, stepped back, and looked at me coolly. "Do you regret the investment?"

"Of course not, but now, with my credit card max'ed out . . ."

"I've got cash in my purse, enough to finance this operation. McGerk needs time to search the house, and the Landmark makes a real production of serving dinner—at least an hour, especially if you take time to ply her with a lot of wine. Round trip to Marquette, driving slowly, another hour. Two hours—does that leave you enough time, McGerk?"

He nodded. "Forty grand'll take up sum space. If it's in th'house, I should be able t'run it down in a coupl'a hours. Do we wanna make this look like a burglary?"

I shook my head. "No. If nothing looks disturbed, she might not check the hiding place for days. We can't predict what she'll do when she finds the money's missing, so the more time that goes by before she's aware that it's gone, the better off we are."

Chris grabbed the manicure scissors again. "Hold still, there's another long hair in your ear."

"Oh, for crissakes . . ."

Maria lived on South Second Street in one of those old frame houses built by the iron miners back in the 1920's. Pastel green siding had been added recently in an attempt to dress up the place, but the house needed more than new siding.

The neighboring houses had neatly cleared, snow-blown paths from the street to the door, but the snow on Maria's path was trampled down by a woman's heeled boots. Apparently there wasn't a man in residence. I knocked and Maria opened the door.

She had shed her bank-teller image for jeweled-frame eyeglasses and blue eye shadow. Her dress—at least one size too small—was the short, black cocktail variety. It had a dangerously low neckline, and

Maria's ample bosom strained and threatened to escape at any moment.

I quickly recovered. "You look stunning tonight."

"Thank you. Come in."

The small living room was overrun with legions of stuffed rabbits. Bunnies of all colors and sizes sat on the sofa, the overstuffed chair, and the TV set.

"What a splendid collection," I remarked.

"Some of them are worth quite a bit of money," Maria confided.

I wondered what she meant by that. Forty thousand dollars could have been hidden in one or more of the larger stuffed animals.

Something stiff and pointed suddenly probed my butt. I jerked my head around to find the biggest Doberman Pinscher I'd ever seen sniffing my posterior.

"Muffin, don't do that," Maria scolded.

I hurriedly moved away from the dog, who interpreted my retreat as a sign of weakness and quickly moved in again, its muzzle now a scant inch from my crotch.

"He always has to investigate strangers," Maria explained.

"Nice Muffin," I said, tentatively putting my hand out to pet the dog.

The Doberman's upper lip instantly slid back to reveal an array of sharp, dagger-like teeth. A deep, raspy sound issued from his throat.

"Don't try to pet him," Maria advised. "Muffin doesn't like petting. Muffin, SIT!"

The dog obediently went into the small dining room and sat on a padded mat which served as his bed. He continued to watch me closely, his huge shoulder muscles quivering in anticipation of getting a command from Maria to spring and tear my throat out.

"They make wonderful watchdogs," Maria said. "A single woman living alone can't be too careful, you know."

"Do you keep him inside, even when you're gone?"

"Oh, yes. Muffin guards all my bunnies. And he never barks, which the neighbors really appreciate."

"Not even if a prowler should come around?"

"No. They say that Dobermans attack silently."

Maria put on her coat and picked up a huge purse with dozens of zippered pockets—another possible hiding place for the money.

My mind worked furiously as we drove toward the highway, trying to think of a way to warn McGerk before he left for Maria's house. Finally, I pulled up to a party-supply store on Third Street.

"Maria, I just remembered a phone call I have to make. I won't be a minute, so why don't you stay comfortable and wait in the car."

Maria agreed. She pulled a makeup bag out of her purse as I left the car.

I went into the store, hurried to the pay phone in the rear, and called McGerk.

"Hello?"

"McGerk, we've got to call it off for tonight."

"Why?"

I lowered my voice to a hoarse whisper. "She's got a watchdog in the house."

"That's okay. I'm good with dogs."

"McGerk, this dog's a killer—a big Doberman. Take it from me, you don't want to meet up with him while you're breaking into the house."

"Where ya callin' from?"

"That party store on Third Street."

"Go on to Marquette an' have dinner. Jus' gimme a li'l extra time, an' I'll handle the mutt."

"You're crazy, McGerk."

"Don' worry 'bout a thing."

"Well, if you manage to get into the house, squeeze the stuffed bunnies."

"The whut?"

"The house is full of stuffed rabbits. The money just might be hidden in any one of them. Check them out by squeezing their stomachs."

McGerk hung up.

I went back to the car cursing McGerk's stupidity about the dog. He was going to mess the whole thing up and probably get himself eaten alive in the process.

19

*M*aria dropped her large purse on the thick carpet, went over to the Sky Room windows, and marveled at the spectacular view of the harbor. "Oh, will you look at that!" The waiter waited patiently for her to return to the table, then deftly slid the highly polished antique chair out to seat her.

"Do you like merlot?" I asked her, noting that the wine list still carried the relatively inexpensive, thirty-dollar-a-bottle label that Chris and I drank in December.

"Oh, yes," she said enthusiastically.

"I imagine, being a good-looking single woman, you must be very popular with the men around here." I'd elected to use flattery to stall for the extra time that McGerk would need to break into the house and deal with the dog.

She smiled teasingly. "Well, I've had my share of boyfriends all right, but I'm pretty particular. I just haven't found the right man yet."

I reached over and took one of her hands in mine. "Well, perhaps your luck is about to change."

Maria tilted her head to bring me into focus through her jeweled bifocals. "Maybe you're right," she said slowly, attempting to sound suggestive.

The wine steward presented the bottle of merlot, and I performed the perfunctory label inspection and taste test. He filled our glasses and drifted away.

Maria was thoroughly enjoying the experience, gazing around at the room's elegant decor. She drained half of the glass of wine in one swallow and placed her hand up to her mouth to suppress a giggle. "This dry winter weather makes me so thirsty."

"So, drink up. A bit of fine wine is in perfect order for such a special occasion," I said with authority, refilling her glass.

She was working on her third glass by the time the waiter arrived. After I placed our dinner order he topped off Maria's wine glass again. I lifted my glass over the table toward her and chuckled slyly. "Here's to good fortune in meeting one another."

Maria misjudged the distance between the two glasses and almost shattered them as she clinked hers against mine. "If I keep on drinking, I'm going to get loose."

"And what happens when you get loose?" I teased, not really wanting to know.

She fixed me with a bright-eyed stare and slowly moistened her lips. "If you're not careful, you may find out."

When the salads arrived, Maria attempted to lift the cherry tomato from the plate to her mouth, balancing it on the tines of her fork. The tomato fell to the floor, bouncing along the carpet like a ground ball. The maitre d' spotted it, rushed over, and scooped it up with the grace of a major-league third-baseman.

"That's why I like coleslaw," Maria remarked irritably. "It doesn't have any of those damned, slippery little tomatoes in it." She put her hand up to her mouth. "Well, excuse *me*. I usually don't use that kind of language."

I emptied the last of the wine into Maria's glass and discretely signaled to the waiter for another bottle. "So tell me," I said, "what do you do when you're on vacation? Travel?"

Maria lost her good humor and took another drink of wine. "Travel? Hell, I've never been any further than Chicago! Could never afford trips. That's gonna change, though."

"And well it should. A vital young woman like yourself should see the world. You've been saving your money, I imagine."

Maria leaned across the table to say something in confidence, then decided that I was too far away. She got to her feet and began sliding her dishes and silver to a place next to mine. Startled, the maitre d' rushed over to help her.

She sat down again and put a heavy hand on my arm. "That's much better."

The wine steward arrived with the fresh bottle and refilled her glass.

"We were talking about you saving your money," I reminded her.

Maria winked slowly and deliberately. "I know how to play heads-up ball, honey, when it comes t'money. Hey, that rhymes."

"You mean that you take advantage of good investment opportunities?"

She laughed at the question. "Taking advantage of investment opportunities—hah, that's good." She lowered her voice. "Let's jus' say that when I spot a chance to fatten my nest egg, I grab it." She carefully aimed her hand at the stem of her wine glass, picked it up, and took a hefty swig.

That clinched it. There was no doubt in my mind that she had the forty thousand dollars. But where? I was frantically trying to figure out how to pry more information out of her when the entrees arrived.

For the next twenty minutes I concentrated on dinner and black coffee, to remain alert and sober. At any moment Maria might start dropping hints about where the money was stashed. At the very least, I needed to get her separated from that big purse long enough to go through it. There was the distinct possibility that I also might need to do some creative ad-libbing when we got back to her house in the event that the Doberman had killed McGerk and left his remains on the living-room carpet.

Maria barely sampled the entree and vegetables, sticking to wine and an occasional roll. She gave me a heavy-lidded, seductive look as she nibbled on a roll.

"Say, stud, whaddaya say we hit the road an' go back to my place?"

I glanced at my watch. McGerk needed a little more time, so I topped off Maria's wine glass again. "They have a great selection of desserts here. You ought to try one."

"T'hell with the desserts," Maria declared loudly, capturing the attention of nearby diners. "I'll give ya dessert when we get home." A hand was stroking my thigh under the table.

"I believe I'll have some of their chocolate mousse," I said brightly. "Are you sure you won't have some?"

"Well . . . if you're gonna be a party pooper. Jus' tell 'em to hold the antlers, ha, ha, ha."

We had dessert and I drank more black coffee while Maria killed the second bottle of wine.

"So, are you going to do some traveling with the proceeds from your investments?"

Maria glowered at me. "I thought this was gonna be a nice romantic evening. Why'd you keep talkin' 'bout money? You wunna them gigolos?"

I began apologizing, but she had already moved on to more pressing matters.

"Gotta go to the li'l girls' room." She tried to pick up her purse, but the sheer mass of it was too great, and she nearly toppled over onto my lap.

I grabbed her elbows to steady her. "That purse looks pretty heavy.

Why don't you go on to the ladies room, and I'll watch it for you."

Maria nodded and lurched off in search of the rest room.

As soon as she was out of sight, I dragged the purse over to my feet and began opening zippers. There were several good-sized compartments, and I searched them all. I discovered a paper sack with a box of twelve prophylactics and a pharmacy receipt bearing today's date. She'd come prepared.

But no forty thousand dollars. I was closing the last zipper when the waiter arrived with the check.

I quickly straightened up, grinning. "You can never find a Kleenex when you need one."

He smiled politely and placed the dinner check on the table.

I picked it up and blinked with astonishment at the amount. Chris hadn't donated enough cash to cover it all. We hadn't figured on the extra bottle of wine.

After performing a quick mental calculation, I added on a very modest tip, then handed the waiter all the cash I had, plus my Hematite First National credit card.

"Subtract the cash from the total and use the credit card for the balance." After this transaction I would be one dollar under the credit-card limit.

Maria returned unsteadily from the rest room. It was time to leave. Two hours had elapsed since I'd picked her up, and, dog or no dog, if McGerk had been able to break into her house and search it, he would have done so by now.

20

*O*nly the console between the front seats of my Oldsmobile prevented Maria from sexually assaulting me during the drive back to Ishpeming. She still managed to reach over and dig her long fingernails into my thigh. I expected to see welts there the next morning.

When we pulled up to her house I dreaded going inside. McGerk might be in there, held at bay by the Doberman, or worse—dead. If by some miracle he had escaped or given up on the break-in, I still had Maria to contend with. For all I knew she might decide to command Muffin to guard the front door while she had her way with me.

After a few unsuccessful attempts, Maria got her key into the lock and pushed the door open.

"Muffin?" she called out sweetly. "We're home."

I stood just inside the front door and looked around nervously but couldn't spot the dog.

"Oh, Muffin, there you are. What's the matter baby? Are you tired?"

Maria had gone into the dining room. The Doberman was lying on his side on the dog bed in the corner. He was totally unresponsive to Maria, not even lifting his head.

She stooped down to pet the dog. His eyes slowly blinked. "Poor baby," she crooned. "We're sorry we woke you up." She petted the dog once more, straightened up and smiled at me. "I'll be right back," she said and headed toward the bedroom.

Maria was too drunk to notice that there was something very wrong with the dog. I edged closer and cautiously bent down over the animal. Had McGerk drugged or poisoned him?

Beer fumes drifted past my nose. There was an inch of flat beer in the dog's water dish next to the cushion. The Doberman watched me but with no hint of savageness. Muffin was drunk on beer—McGerk's signature, alright.

The bedroom door opened and Maria flitted out in a scanty negligee, her silhouette outlined through the filmy material, large breasts bouncing around like a pair of romping otters.

"I'll make us a nightcap," she said, heading for the kitchen. "I don't usually keep liquor in the house, but I've still got some peppermint schnapps left over from Christmas."

"Sounds good to me," I replied absently.

While Maria busied herself in the kitchen with the drinks, my eyes darted around the living and dining rooms for any possible clue to suggest that McGerk's search had been successful. Nothing appeared to be disturbed. The numerous stuffed rabbits stared innocently at me, just as they had before we left.

Soft breasts pressed into my back, and Maria thrust a glass into my hand. "Why don' we adjourn to the bedroom where we won't disturb poor sleepy ol' Muffin," she coaxed from behind me.

The last thing I wanted to do was to get anywhere near a bed with Maria, but I had to look around the bedroom, so I followed her.

Incredibly, there were more stuffed rabbits—at least a dozen—lounging on the double bed. With one swipe of her free hand, Maria sent the bunnies flying in all directions. She sat down heavily on the edge of the bed and patted a spot next to her. "Let's jus' sit here a li'l ol' minute and sip our nightcaps."

I sat down next to her, took a sip of the schnapps, and gasped for air. It tasted like jet fuel.

Without further conversation, Maria swung her feet onto the bed and with surprising strength grabbed my necktie and pulled me down on top of her. The peppermint schnapps slopped all over the front of my shirt.

She planted a long wet kiss on my lips. I started to resist but found that if I turned my head back and forth, as you might do in a truly passionate kiss, the position was ideal for scanning the room. The kiss lingered on and on while I inspected the dresser, the open closet, and the floor. Nothing seemed to be disturbed.

After a long minute, I unpuckered and slowly raised my head, wondering how I was going to avoid the next phase of Maria's sexual agenda. She didn't stir. Her eyes were closed and her breathing had become deep and regular. I remained motionless for minutes, looking silently down on her.

She began to snore.

I carefully got off the bed, crept out, and looked around the living room again. McGerk had either been very neat with his search or hadn't performed it at all. It was even possible that in the process of getting the Doberman drunk he had been bitten badly enough to require medical attention.

Toenails scrabbling the linoleum on the dining-room floor sent an icy flash of terror down my spine. Muffin was struggling to get to his feet. Letting out a half-howl, half-snarl, he came at me.

But the large dog still wasn't sober, and his body wouldn't respond to the attack. He charged, but his hind legs crabbed and wobbled badly as he slid sideways, losing momentum.

"Muffin, SIT!" I yelled in desperation.

The command seemed to register in the Doberman's muddled brain. He turned and staggered back to his cushion in the dining room where he sat and watched me, drunkenly dejected over his failure to rip me apart.

Heart pounding, breathing in ragged gasps, I stood staring at the dog. There was something out of sync.

Muffin's cushion wasn't padded anymore. It was totally flat.

Sighing with relief, I hurried out the door.

Back at my apartment, the stacks of currency on the coffee table were considerably larger than the ones that McGerk and I had counted after the robbery. McGerk was fingering fifties, counting aloud while Chris tallied them on my pocket calculator.

"The dog's bed, huh?" I said.

McGerk grinned. "Y'got sharp eyes."

Chris came over and kissed me. "Gawd, what's that awful smell?"

"Peppermint schnapps."

She sniffed my shirt, then inspected it more closely. Somehow, during the struggle on the bed, Maria had succeeded in planting three or four lipstick imprints on my shirt.

Chris scowled at me. "Kissing you on the *chest*? This was supposed to be a dinner date, mister."

"I didn't know if McGerk had gotten the money or not, so I wanted to look around inside the house. There was a struggle on the bed, but *nothing*, I mean *nothing*, happened. In fact, she fell asleep before anything *could* happen."

"Our boy here is th'last of the red-hot lovers," McGerk commented dryly to Chris.

That broke the tension and everyone laughed. With the money in our hands, we felt better than we had in days.

"I asked her too many questions about money over dinner tonight," I said. "She's going to wake up, find the forty thousand missing, and immediately assume that I took it. There's no telling what she'll do."

"Whut *can* she do?" McGerk argued. "If she's smart, she'll keep her mouth shut. Besides, we're takin' it in to th'bank first thing in th'morning."

He looked at his watch. "Which reminds me, get outta that suit an' tie, lover-boy. We gotta go shoppin' fer one more snowmobile."

21

"**B**orrowing" another snowmobile for our second reverse robbery attempt wasn't going to be easy. At one-thirty Wednesday morning McGerk and I, with his truck and trailer, were parked across the highway from the fourth motel we'd reconnoitered in the past two hours. The bank-robbery publicity had people on edge, especially snowmobilers. Nervous motel owners in the area had now placed night guards in their parking lots.

McGerk, peering through the windshield, jabbed his finger toward the motel lot. "Y'see that? Somebody's smokin' a cigarette in that Ford truck parked down at th'end. I jus' seen th'cigarette tip flare up."

I stared out at where he was pointing. "I don't see a thing." All I could make out were the dark blobs of parked cars and pickup trucks.

"Think he's got a gun?" I asked.

"I dunno, but we ain't gonna find out." McGerk grunted, starting up the truck.

"I can't believe we're doing this for the third time," I said as we drove down the highway. "If the *motels* are that closely guarded, what's the *bank* going to be like?"

McGerk didn't seem concerned. "Inna million years they won't figgur on us comin' back a third time. Besides, this time we're goin' in earlier. Watch 'em open up at nine o'clock, see if there's any cops around, an' then move in."

"We still don't have a sled."

"I got an idea 'bout that," McGerk said.

Minutes later McGerk turned off the highway and pulled into the darkened back parking lot of Arctic Land, the biggest snowmobile dealer in the area.

"We're going to steal a *new* sled?" I exclaimed.

"Why not?" McGerk said, easing the truck up to the back door and killing the engine and headlights.

I laughed nervously. "We're really moving up in the world."

McGerk removed some rubber gloves, a small plastic case, and two small narrow-beam flashlights from the glove compartment. He handed me a pair of gloves and a flashlight. "This place don't open till 9 A.M. By th'time they figgur out a sled's missin', we'll have already been at th'bank an' gone. Somebody'll find th'sled right after we ditch it."

Standing at the back door I asked, "What if there's a burglar alarm?"

McGerk shook his head. "I been here lots'a times waitin' fer 'em to open in th'morning, t'get stuff from their parts department. Th'guy openin' up just puts a key in this door. Doesn't shut off any alarm inside."

McGerk removed a few angled, wire-like instruments from his case and tried a couple in the lock. In a matter of seconds he had the door open. We went inside. Playing the flashlight beams in front of us, we navigated down a dark corridor, finally emerging into the showroom overlooking the highway. The headlights of a passing car cast streaks of light across a long row of new snowmobiles sitting on the showroom floor.

McGerk strode over to the front window and closed the vertical blinds so our flashlights wouldn't be seen by passing motorists. He walked along the row of snowmobiles, playing the tiny beam of light on each sled.

He stopped at one. "Jeezuz!" he whispered reverently. "I heard 'bout this baby but never thought I'd see it."

It was some type of snowmobile—with skis and a track—but it was unlike any I'd seen. The sled was wider and lower with a flat, wedge-shaped nose that drooped like a stealth fighter. The air intakes—one on each side—were big and nostril-like, giving it the appearance of a large, reptilian monster.

"What is it?"

McGerk, ignoring my question, opened the hood and played the light on the engine. "Lookit that. Three 100-millimeter cylinders, triple 88 billet stroker crankshaft, 250 foot-pounds of torque . . . this sucker's got 325 horsepower."

The engine was enormous, covered with a jungle of wire, tubing, and ducts. It didn't look a bit like the engine in McGerk's MACH 1.

"325 horsepower? I didn't know they even made *200* horsepower engines for snowmobiles."

"Normally, they don't," McGerk replied.

"What do they call this thing?"

McGerk lowered the hood and played the flashlight beam along the machine's jet-black chassis. Small white letters read PROJECT X. "This sled's strictly research—one of a few built in a design shop near Eagle River, Wisconsin, out in th'middle of th'woods fer security."

"What's it doing here? Is it for sale?"

"Nah . . . must be on tour. Sled dealers like t'get these prototypes on loan fer a few days, just to put in th'showroom to whet th'customers' appetites."

"What does the X stand for?" I asked.

McGerk smiled. "Don'cha remember yer high-school algebra? X is th'unknown? That's whut this is—th'unknown."

"Unknown what?"

"Unknown speed," McGerk replied, lovingly caressing the handlebars with his gloved hand. "Nobody knows fer sure how fast it'll go."

"Faster than your MACH 1?"

McGerk laughed. "Hell yes, *much* faster."

I was beginning to get edgy standing around in the dark building. "This is all very interesting, but let's grab a sled and get out of here. For all we know, they might have a night watchman making rounds."

"We're gonna take this one."

"The *X*? For crissake, look at the seat. It's a one-man sled. Both of us can't get on it."

But McGerk wasn't about to argue. "We'll manage. I gotta have this sled."

"McGerk, this isn't a shopping spree. We only need the sled for ten—fifteen minutes tops—then we're going to ditch it." I pointed to the snowmobile next in line. "How about this one? A touring sled with a nice big seat."

But McGerk was already checking the X's fuel gauge. "That's the trouble with ripping off sleds from the showroom floor. They never have much gas. I'll get that full can of gas out of the truck. You go over to that far wall an' pick out sum nice things fer us to wear this morning."

While McGerk fueled and checked out the prototype sled, I began pawing through Arctic Land's extensive inventory of clothing. Doing it by flashlight slowed me down, but I got caught up in the excitement of being able to pick out anything without regard to price. It was like a winter clearance sale with 100 percent off.

I selected expensive black-leather, fleece-lined jackets with matching bib pants made by Skidoo and sleek helmets—also in black—with double-lens face shields. I grabbed two of everything. McGerk and I, and the X, would be totally color-coordinated when we made our final public appearance at the bank.

On another wall they displayed two-way electronic communicators, allowing snowmobilers to converse with one another above the engine noise—a Ni-cad battery power/transmitter unit with antenna attached to the edge of one helmet, and earphones and mikes mounted with Velcro on the inside of the helmets. I quickly scanned the instruction booklet and rigged up both helmets.

Next to a salesman's desk was a large, wheeled cart, piled high with brochures. I emptied the cart, pulled it over, and loaded it with clothing.

McGerk finished with the X and motioned to my cart heaped high with gear. "Throw that stuff in the truck, bring th'cart back inside, an' then take off. Like last time, drive down th'road an' wait fer me. If anybody should hear this sled start up an' come runnin', we wanna have th'truck a long ways away from here. I'll be there in a coupl'a minutes."

I drove the truck and trailer about a mile down an adjacent side road and parked. Even at that distance I heard the X's engine the moment McGerk hot-wired it.

A quarter mile away, its lone headlight popped into view as the prototype sled rounded the final curve. The light charged toward me like a shrieking meteor reentering the atmosphere. At the last second, McGerk slammed on the brakes, sending up a towering sheet of snow over the truck and me as the powerful machine skidded to a stop.

"GAWDAMN!" he yelled exuberantly. "This thing is somethin' *else!*"

I had the trailer platform tilted down on the snow-packed roadway.

McGerk drove the X up onto the trailer and killed the engine and headlight. We quickly threw the tarp over the machine, cinched it down, and drove off.

We were becoming experts at stealing snowmobiles. That is, if what we had just stolen could even be classified as a snowmobile.

We stopped at my apartment to pick up the cash—the twenty-six hundred hidden in the Grape-Nuts box and the forty thousand taken earlier from the Doberman's bed—and headed over to McGerk's place. By the time we got the X stowed into his garage, altered the paste-up note, and packaged the money, it was four in the morning. There was no point in returning to my apartment, so I bedded down on McGerk's sofa for a few hours sleep.

But I lay there, wide awake. When I smelled cigarette smoke, I glanced through the open door into McGerk's bedroom. His cigarette flared in the darkness as he inhaled deeply.

I switched on a living-room lamp and called toward the bedroom. "Didn't your mother ever teach you not to smoke in bed?"

"Ya want sum coffee?" he asked.

"Might as well."

McGerk got out of bed and I followed him into the small kitchen.

While the coffee was brewing, McGerk stared through the frosty kitchen window into the winter darkness as he finished his cigarette. Without turning, he said, "Whaddaya gonna do after today?"

"You mean if we don't get caught?"

"Aw, we ain't gonna get caught."

"I hope you're right. Anyway, after you left Monday night Chris and I talked for a long time. If we can get that money back to the bank today, and if the heat dies down, and if the police really put the case in cold storage, then maybe there's hope for the future. Of course, I've got to give up that apartment and sell the furniture to make a lump-sum payment on the credit card. Then I'll try to work out some arrangement with the bank so I can whittle down the rest of the balance with whatever I can save out of my flooring-mill check."

"Ya gonna move in with Chris?"

"Yeah, I guess so. I don't want to jeopardize her position at the university, but she pointed out that as long as I'm not sneaking out every morning, it's no big deal. We both agree that it's too early to think long term, like getting married. As the saying goes, we'll take it one day at a time. Meanwhile, I'm going to get back to writing that book I started."

I remembered that McGerk's plans after the big haul were far more ambitious than mine. "How about you? What are you going to do?"

"Prob'ly sell th'garage an' try t'pay off that new equipment, an' then move outta here. Maybe go down t'Milwaukee or Chicago an' get a job in one of them big auto dealerships takin' th'kinks outta new cars."

That jarred me. "Move? Why? You're a good mechanic. You can get a job at any garage around here."

McGerk poured the coffee and handed me a cup. "I don't wanna move, but I been my own boss too long. I go to work fer somebody else around here, people'll always say I wasn't good enough t'make it on my own. Don' think I'd be able to put up with that. Too proud, I guess."

"That's stupid," I said angrily, not knowing why I was getting upset. "Just because you can't bear the thought of working for someone else, you're going to move away from your hometown—the place you've lived all your life?"

McGerk didn't understand why I was getting mad either. "What th'hell do you care? You gotta nice girl—owns a big house—and she's invitin' ya t'move in with her. Who've I got? *Nobody*! Ain't nuthin' keepin' me here."

"You've got me and Chris. We're all friends, aren't we?"

McGerk smiled sadly. "Yeah, we are, an' I couldn't ask fer two better friends. But that ain't quite th'same as whut *you* got, is it?"

"You haven't had a girlfriend in awhile, have you?"

McGerk shook his head, continuing to stare out the window.

"Didn't you ever get serious about any of the women you've taken out?"

He lit up another cigarette, took a long drag, and exhaled smoke on the frosty window pane. "Think I could'a gotten serious 'bout Maria, but she wanted sumbody with cleaner hands, I guess."

"Maria? You mean to tell me that of all the women you've taken out that Maria Grazzelli would've been your woman of choice?" I laughed, and then wished I hadn't.

McGerk drilled me with a hard, flat stare. "Whut's so funny? Jus' 'cause she turned out to be a crook like us?"

I didn't reply.

McGerk dropped the cigarette butt into the dregs of his coffee. "Let's see if we kin still get a few hours sleep before we get movin'."

22

For an hour McGerk and I had been waiting, just within the edge of the woods across the highway from the Hematite First National Bank. With bank robberies foremost on everyone's mind, we'd decided that the safest strategy was to keep an eye on the bank for a full hour before it opened to spot any sign of police surveillance activity.

The wait was brutal. We were crammed together like Siamese twins on the small seat of the snowmobile. Sitting outside in U.P. winter weather for any length of time will freeze your butt, no matter how warmly you're dressed. There wasn't any snow falling, so getting off the sled to move around and get warm would have left telltale footprints, providing clues for the police.

There was no place to stash anything, other than on our bodies. I had all the money—over forty-two thousand dollars—bundled up in plastic Baggies and crammed into the many large zippered pockets on my jacket. McGerk wore binoculars around his neck to observe activity at the bank. Stuffed in the big pockets of his jacket were the paste-up note, assorted tools, and the precious small thermos of coffee.

I tapped McGerk on the shoulder. "Give me the coffee."

Grumbling, he fished out the thermos. "Go easy on that—there ain't much left."

I unscrewed the plastic cup and shakily poured hot coffee into it.

Embracing the cup with both gloved hands, I sipped the steaming brew.

McGerk trained his binoculars on the bank again. "Here comes Arne Laxso—fifteen minutes early. He's alone."

"We gotta sit here for another fifteen minutes?"

"Uh-huh. Banks never open early."

The minutes ticked by. Finally, more cars pulled into the parking lot; the tellers were arriving. McGerk carefully identified each person as they entered the bank.

"Here comes yer date from last night," he announced.

Maria Grazzelli slipped and slid across the packed snow in the back parking lot, her shaky equilibrium probably due to a hangover.

"Think she knows th'money's gone from the dog's bed?" McGerk asked.

I smiled in spite of the cold. "I don't know, but she's going to figure it out real quick when we walk in and plunk down forty-two grand on the counter."

McGerk kept the glasses trained on the front door for another few minutes. "Okay, they jus' unlocked th'front door." He pulled his ski mask and visor down and turned on the power to the two-way communication unit.

His voice crackled in my ears. "Do you read me?"

I spoke into the mike mounted near my mouth. "Yes, do you read *me*?" I felt like the co-pilot on a bombing run.

"Loud and clear," McGerk answered. "Let's go."

He punched the electric starter on the X. Even with my head sealed in the padded helmet, the powerful engine was deafening. I gripped McGerk's waist tightly as we surged out of the woods.

McGerk steered the snowmobile across the highway toward the bank, his voice in my earphones, "This time we don' any take chances. We're both goin' in."

He braked to a stop at the front door and left the engine running. We hopped off and entered the bank.

This time no one was fooled. Two helmeted snowmobilers dressed in black meant only one thing. First, one teller screamed—then another.

Arne Laxso charged out of his office. "WHAT THE HELL . . . *AGAIN*?"

A big concern was that someone working in the bank might be armed now—in particular, Laxso, the manager. I held up my left hand, indicating to Laxso that he should remain right where he was. With my right hand stuffed in the jacket pocket, I jabbed my forefinger threateningly toward him as though I had him covered with a gun. Laxso stopped and glared at me.

We were intent on getting this over with as quickly as possible. McGerk produced the paste-up note while I began removing Baggies of cash from the zippered pockets. We moved toward the teller next to Maria.

Maria saw the note in McGerk's gloved hand and the bundles of cash I had in my hand. She reached below the counter and came up with a chrome-plated revolver.

"YOU DIRTY, ROTTEN, SMOOTHTALKING, SONOFABITCH!" She planted her elbows on the counter, held the gun with both hands, took dead aim, and fired.

McGerk's cry of pain rang in my ears. He spun around and fell to the floor, the note skittering away.

I dropped down next to him. "Where are you hit?" I asked frantically, forgetting the strategy to remain silent.

McGerk's voice in my earphones sounded surprised. "She shot me."

"Where are you hit?" I repeated.

A floor tile next to his hip exploded. Maria was still shooting.

McGerk tried to scramble to his feet, but his right leg buckled beneath him. A hole in his leather-clad thigh was oozing blood. I plunged my gloved hands under his arms and—all the while not daring to glance back at Maria—dragged him through the front door.

The getaway was a big problem now. The X was ready to go, engine idling, but McGerk was shot and I hadn't been checked out on the strange machine.

Suddenly, McGerk struggled free of my grasp. He hopped crazily over to the snowmobile and threw his wounded leg across the seat, motioning for me to get on behind him. He pointed toward the highway, his voice barking in my earphones.

"COPS!"

Fifty yards away, a blue four-wheel-drive Michigan State Police unit, bubble light flashing, was blocking our access to the highway. A trailer loaded with two blue snowmobiles was hitched to it. Two officers in padded navy blue jumpsuits were already out of the vehicle, one hurrying to the trailer and the other looking at us and drawing his service revolver.

"GET ON!" McGerk roared.

I jumped aboard as McGerk gunned the X toward the rear of the bank parking lot.

The lot was enclosed on three sides by a cinder-block wall. All winter long, plows clearing the lot had pushed the snow to the far end, creating an eight-foot snowbank that completely buried the rear wall. The tall bank of snow sloped at a sixty-degree angle. Our only possible avenue of escape was to climb the bank with the snowmobile.

McGerk made a sharp turn at the back corner of the lot and for an instant sped parallel to the snowbank. "HANG ON!" he commanded as the snowmobile began scaling the snowbank diagonally. The X tilted dangerously to the right as we tore up the side like a fly scooting across a wall. I hung on to McGerk for dear life.

The X slowed momentarily when we reached the top and then dove down the other side, slewing, bucking, and jumping down the loose snow.

We landed in a meadow behind the Hematite Bank but found still more problems. Huge granite boulders unearthed during the construction of the bank building dotted the meadow. McGerk skillfully dodged several of them, but to avoid an almost certain collision we had no recourse but to skirt around the walled parking lot and head back toward the highway.

We now faced a deep drainage ditch that paralleled the road. McGerk plunged the snowmobile to the bottom of the ditch, raising a monstrous cloud of snow. Then—engine screaming—the X climbed up the steep incline onto the shoulder of Highway 41.

I looked back toward the bank's driveway a hundred yards behind us. The police snowmobiles were off the trailer now and the two officers were climbing aboard.

"They're gonna come after us on those sleds," I shouted.

"Tell me sumthin' I don' know," McGerk snapped.

A split second later the state police troopers were charging after us at a high rate of speed. McGerk goosed the throttle on the X, almost losing me as the machine rose off its skis and accelerated sharply. I wrapped my arms tighter around McGerk as we sped east on the shoulder of the highway.

Looking over McGerk's shoulder, I could see the speedometer. We were rocketing along at well over eighty miles an hour, on the shoulder, passing cars on the right side like they were standing still.

Yet the police snowmobiles were staying with us, only about two hundred yards to the rear.

Reading my thoughts, McGerk's voice crackled in my earphones, "This sled's faster, but we're carrying two and they're only carryin' one."

We were heading down the sweeping curve toward West Ishpeming. A quarter mile away three police cruisers had set up a roadblock across the highway, waiting for us. Several officers were leaning across the hoods of their cars, arms extended.

"They got guns out!" McGerk barked, slamming on the brakes hard. We made a sharp, skidding U-turn in the middle of the highway and headed back toward Ishpeming, riding the opposite shoulder. The snowmobile troopers did the same and stayed tight on our tail.

"McGerk—I still have the money."

"Ya didn't leave it at th'bank?"

"When Maria fired that first shot, I got rattled. I wasn't thinking and I shoved the money back into my jacket."

McGerk jerked his head around to check on our pursuers. In addition to the two snowmobiles, we had also picked up the three police cruisers. "Well, at th'rate this chase is goin', th'money ain't gonna be our biggest problem. Th'cops'll have both th'cash an' us in another minute or two."

"Maybe not," I said, pulling my gloves off and taking out one of the Baggies filled with money. I opened it up and pulled out a big handful of fifty-dollar bills. Holding the bills high above my head, I slowly released them into the wind.

The results were immediate. The sharp-eyed driver of a big logging rig heading in the opposite direction spotted the money blowing around. He hit the brakes but too hard. The loaded trailer jackknifed on the slushy road surface, snapping the chains holding the big load and spilling logs all over the highway. Several cars following the truck swerved to avoid the logs and spun into the path of the police vehicles. Brakes screeched and fenders crumpled.

We reached the top of the hill. At the traffic light we made a sudden left turn onto North Second Street and flew past the Ishpeming Cemetery. I looked behind us again. Now there was only one police snowmobile following us.

23

*F*urther north, Second Street became Deer Lake Road, a tricky two-laner twisting through the woods for several miles. The road was plowed following an overnight snowfall, but no sand or salt had been put down yet. At that moment, Deer Lake Road was an ideal snowmobile run.

McGerk's voice came through my earphones, "I know this road pretty well. Let's see how well that cop behind us knows it."

The X jolted forward. We rocketed into a blind curve with McGerk leaning his upper body far out to his left to shift the center of gravity. Numbed beyond fear, I followed suit.

We tore up Deer Lake Road at unbelievable speeds, leaning so precariously into the sharp curves that it seemed our knees and elbows were only inches from the snowy roadway. My stomach floated nauseatingly every time we became airborne after hurtling over the top of a hill.

On one rare straightaway I looked back. The state trooper was nowhere in sight.

"Do you suppose he turned back?" I asked.

No reply. I glanced down at McGerk's thigh—covered with blood.

"McGerk, are you okay?" I nudged him in the ribs. "McGerk, say something."

I touched his right arm; his hand flopped from the throttle and the powerful snowmobile immediately slowed down.

Remarkably, McGerk's left hand was still steering the machine. I supported his left elbow, steadying the arm while the X continued to lose speed. As soon as it stopped, I jumped off.

Before I could grab him, McGerk slumped over and fell onto the roadway. The snow beneath his leg instantly turned bright red.

I knelt down and opened the visor on his helmet. "How do you feel?" A stupid question—he looked like hell.

Wispy vapors floated from McGerk's mouth as he took shallow breaths. "I been better. We shake that cop?"

I took my helmet off and listened. "I don't know—I can't hear him. Listen, we've got to get you to a hospital and have a doctor look at that leg."

McGerk glared. "An' turn ourselves in after all this? Hell, no! Look, there's a guy in Ishpeming—in his eighties—use'ta be a bootlegger. Brings his car to th'garage alla time an' tells me stories 'bout how he fixed up gunshot wounds in th'old days. We'll sneak into town and go an' see him."

"McGerk, you want to go back into Ishpeming on a stolen sled—with every cop in the county looking for us—and have some old bootlegger operate on your leg? That's crazy!"

McGerk lifted his head and glanced at his wounded leg. "Why'd she shoot me? I know we had a helluva fight th'last time I took 'er out, but she didn't haf'ta shoot me."

"I'll bet she wanted to shoot *me*," I said. "She must think that I took the money from the dog's bed after she passed out. When she spotted all that cash in my hand this morning she knew that I was one of the bank robbers, but with the helmets and masks on she didn't know who was who. You had the note in your hand like I did the two other times, and that's why you got shot."

McGerk nodded weakly. "I bet she was gonna come lookin' fer

you on her lunch hour with that gun. Always said that women're more dangerous than men."

We heard a snowmobile coming up fast on the road.

"It's that state trooper," I said.

McGerk struggled around on the snow, trying to get to his feet, but was too weak and fell back onto his elbows.

"Take it easy," I said. "Give it up. Let the cop radio for an ambulance to take you to a hospital."

With superhuman effort, McGerk, groaning, got to his feet. "If yer happy t'spend th'next ten to fifteen years in a five-by-ten cell, then that might be good advice. Get on th'sled."

"Then, I'll drive," I said, putting on my helmet. "Can you hang on?"

McGerk thought for a second, then weakly nodded.

"How are we going to get back?" I asked, helping him onto the snowmobile seat. That trooper is between us and town."

"The Dead River."

"What?"

McGerk motioned north with his head. "Jus' up ahead there's the Dead River Storage Basin—a reservoir. It's wide an' frozen an' goes east fer several miles. Mebbe on the ice, with this hot sled, you kin outrun that cop an' get back t'town. Let's go—I'll show ya th'way."

I got on the seat in front of him and we took off. Even with two on board, I had trouble adapting to the quick acceleration of the prototype sled.

A mile up the road, McGerk pointed off to the right toward a collection of summer cabins, roofs laden with snow. "Go between those camps."

I carefully maneuvered the snowmobile off the road and plunged into the deep snow between the cabins. On the other side was the Dead River Storage Basin.

We paused at the frozen shore and listened. The trooper's

snowmobile sounded closer.

McGerk's voice snapped in my earphones. "Let's go!"

I steered the X out onto the snow-covered ice, opened the throttle wide, and headed east. The powerful machine threw back a huge rooster tail of loose snow as we sped down the basin.

"That cop—he jus' came out on th'ice," McGerk said, looking back. "He's 'bout three, four hundred yards behind us. Let's get a move on."

We were already doing sixty-five, and as I had discovered at Teal Lake, that was plenty fast on loose snow, but I gunned the throttle harder.

The X's engine howled, and the machine rose up and flew. The incredibly stiff wind forced me to take a near-horizontal position, causing my helmet to rap against the handlebars every time the big sled bounced off the snow.

A black speck on the horizon in front of us exploded in size—an ice-fishing shack. As we shot past, I caught a snapshot glimpse of a lone fisherman gaping at us, open-mouthed.

We ain't losin' th'cop!" McGerk said.

I pressed the throttle to the limit. The wind and engine noise merged into one steady deafening roar.

I risked a glimpse down at the speedometer, but the needle was vibrating too badly. When I looked up I saw the big log—half covered with snow and stuck in the ice—directly in front of us.

I was airborne, then skidding, bouncing, and rolling across the snow-covered ice for a long distance. One numbing slam onto the ice wrenched my helmet off. My leg landed under me at an awkward angle and tremendous pain shot up my spine.

The last thing I remember was seeing a fifty-dollar bill floating down to rest on the snow near my head.

❄

24

I couldn't recall the exact moment I really woke up, since I was drifting in and out of consciousness for what seemed like a very long time. The first thing that registered was the gray, winter daylight seeping through draped windows to the left of my bed. I knew I was in a hospital room. The bed had aluminum side rails, and a plastic bag mounted on a pole held some kind of fluid that was dripping into me. Forked tips of an oxygen tube were stuck in my nose. I just didn't know which hospital or how I got there.

My right leg bulged beneath the blanket. I carefully reached down and fingered a cast that began just below my knee. The reaching caused sharp pain in my ribs which were tightly wrapped in layers of tape. Feeling pressure in my head, I gingerly patted some kind of dressing mounted there. The leg, my head, and my ribs didn't hurt if I lay still. I was probably on some kind of painkiller. What in hell had happened to me?

The nightstand was bare—no telephone, flowers, or get-well cards. Apparently I hadn't had any visitors. Visitors? I couldn't even remember any of my *friends*! Did I *have* any friends? Vague images of Southern California flickered through my mind but little else.

A long, pale blue, full-length curtain hanging from a curved ceiling track surrounded most of the bed and blocked off the inner half of the room. I craned my neck but couldn't find a button to ring for a nurse. I felt panicky. I had to find out what happened and why I couldn't remember anything.

Newspapers rustled on the other side of the curtain.

"Hello, who's there?" I called, creating another sharp pain in my ribs.

The curtain slid back, and a tall, young police officer nodded somberly. "I'll call the nurse's station. They wanted to know when you came around."

The sight of the cop sent little chills of terror skittering up my spine, but I didn't know why.

He squatted down next to a telephone lying on the carpet next to the door, punched in three numbers, said a few words, and hung up. Getting up, he pushed the curtain back further, exposing another bed. "Your buddy's asleep, but you're allowed to chat with him when he wakes up."

I stared hard at the sleeping figure in the other bed. It was McGerk. He looked different with his stubble gone and someone had given him a close, almost-military-style haircut. He had several ugly scrape marks on his nose, and his left arm was in a cast. But where did I know McGerk from? I couldn't remember.

Next to the door a small open closet was filled with black leather snowmobile jackets and bib pants that were all torn up. Yellow tags marked "EVIDENCE," in bold black letters, were attached to everything.

In one sudden jolt, everything came rushing back to me.

"McGerk, wake up!"

McGerk's eyes popped open, staring at the ceiling.

"Over here," I said.

Grimacing with pain, he slowly turned his head to look at me. "'Bout time ya woke up."

"Where are we?" I asked.

"Ishpeming Hospital."

"How long have we been here?"

"Cops brought us in on Wednesday. Today's Friday."

"Then, we're in custody, right?"

McGerk snorted a short, humorless laugh and said to the trooper sitting in a chair by the door. "Hear whut my friend said? Wants t'know if we're in custody. Should I tell him 'bout th'long vacation you guys got planned fer us once we feel better? Where'ja say we're goin'? Florida?"

The young officer just smiled.

McGerk scowled at me. "Do me a favor an' don't take me on any more snowmobile rides."

"Oh, that's cute. You were the guy who talked me into taking it up in the first place." My right leg in the cast was starting to itch, but there was nothing I could do about it.

A severe-looking, heavyset nurse bustled through the door but was immediately halted by the trooper who produced a metal-detector wand. He ran it quickly around her stout torso.

"Again, for crying out loud?" she snapped. "You must enjoy that."

"Sorry, regulations."

"When kin I get a pack of cigarettes?" McGerk asked the nurse.

"You've already asked me that," she replied, dismissing the subject. She slapped a blood-pressure cuff on my arm and punched up the pressure.

"What's wrong with me?" I asked her.

"Keep quiet till I've finished with this." The hospital staff obviously didn't reserve their best bedside manner for county prisoners.

The nurse logged the blood pressure on my chart and checked the fluid level in the bag. "The doctor will be along in a minute. He'll answer all your questions." She left the room.

"What kind of shape are you in?" I asked McGerk.

"Whut kind'a shape you *think* I'm in after ya ran th'sled over that gawdamn log at two hunnerd miles an hour."

"Hey, I wanted to surrender, remember?"

After a moment McGerk added, "Gotta busted-up arm an' my back hurts like hell, not to mention th'bullet hole in my leg."

A doctor arrived, received the metal-detector check from the trooper, and came over to my bed. He shone a pencil flashlight into my eyes and listened to my heart.

Anticipating questions, he said, "You've got a mild concussion; you were fortunate considering that you lost your helmet during the accident. As you've no doubt noticed, you also have a broken leg and cracked ribs. At the speed that the state police say you were traveling, I'd say you're lucky to be alive."

"How long will it take for all this to heal?" I asked. Everything was starting to ache now.

The doctor looked surprised. "What's the rush? These accommodations are much better than what you can expect after you recover." He examined McGerk, made some notes that went into a file folder on the back of the door, and then left.

I asked McGerk, "Do you think Chris knows where we are?"

He pointed to the trooper sitting at the door. "Our friend here let me look at yesterday's newspaper. We were th'headline story—even had a picture of th'hospital on the front page. *Everybody* knows where we are."

"Do you think she's been here?" I was anxious to find out if the police knew about Chris's involvement, but I couldn't mention that with the trooper in the room.

McGerk shook his head. "Dunno . . . probabl'y. But they're not lettin' any visitors in. Outside of our twenny-four-hour guard here, even th'cops haven't come 'round fer questioning."

The nurse returned and without a word removed the intravenous tube from my arm and the oxygen tube from my nose. An aide followed, bringing in breakfast trays—juice, toast, and coffee. My jaw must have taken a pretty good whack during the accident, because chewing hurt like hell.

During the next hour there were several knocks on the door. Each time, our guard went out and authoritatively informed people that no one was allowed in the room. One brash TV cameraman tried to push his way in, hoping to grind off some quick footage of the bank robbers, but he was unceremoniously shoved back out into the hallway.

The trooper returned, clearly annoyed, straightening his sharply pressed uniform. "Media people. They think 'NO VISITORS' signs don't apply to them."

The next knock was more commanding. The trooper jumped up from his chair, jerked the door open, and began barking his "no visitors" litany. He was immediately interrupted. The visitor apparently was no stranger to law-enforcement personnel. A brief, sharp-voiced conversation took place in the hallway, and a moment later our guard escorted a well-dressed, middle-aged man into the room.

"This gentleman claims that he's been engaged to represent you."

Puzzled, McGerk and I glanced at one another.

The man made a dismissing motion with his hand toward the door, saying to the police officer. "A little privacy, if you please."

The trooper ran the metal-detector wand over our visitor and inspected the contents of his leather briefcase before reluctantly stepping out of the room. The man immediately produced business cards, handing one to each of us.

"Abraham Glick—attorney at law—at your service," he announced.

Glick had all the trappings of a high-priced lawyer. His short, well-fed frame was outfitted in an expensive, charcoal gray pin-stripe suit and Italian shoes. A gold Rolex watch gleamed on his hairy wrist. Clearly, his receding dark hair had been styled by someone who charged a lot more than a U.P. barber.

McGerk inspected the business card with suspicion. "We didn' hire no lawyer."

Glick smiled. "I know. Perhaps I stretched the truth a bit with the police officer at the door, but you'll either have to engage an attorney or the court will provide one for you. Trust me, choosing one yourself is a better bet."

Glick's card had a Detroit address. "We can't *afford* an attorney, especially one from Detroit," I said.

"You certainly can't afford *me*," Glick replied dryly. "My normal fee, for, say three weeks, would exceed your entire haul from that bank robbery—assuming you did it, of course."

"Then, why are you here?"

"I'm willing to take your cases on a pro bono basis."

McGerk frowned. "Pro bono—whazzat?"

"It means there'll be no charge for my services."

I was dumbfounded. "Why?"

Glick opened his briefcase, took out a newspaper, and handed it to me. "The *Detroit Free Press*—look at the Statewide News on page 5B."

I leafed through the second section of the newspaper. The piece was headlined "U.P. Bank Robbers Have Change of Heart." The story described how two robbers had held up the Hematite First National Bank in Ishpeming, taken forty-two thousand dollars, and escaped on stolen snowmobiles. But the amount of money taken apparently didn't satisfy the robbers and they returned to the bank on the following Monday, trying to score an even bigger haul. This time, however, they were foiled by a customer. Their attempts at pulling off a big heist were so unsuccessful that on Wednesday—according to the note left in the bank by the robbers—they decided to return all of the money and forget the whole thing. But they couldn't even get that right. A bank teller, thinking it was a third robbery attempt, produced a revolver and wounded one of the inept crooks. The two fled from the bank, forgetting their note and also forgetting to leave the money. The article closed with the snowmobile chase, the accident, and the capture.

I gave the newspaper back. Glick handed it to McGerk, who after reading it, threw it to the floor in disgust. "They don't even know whut th'hell went on." The sudden moves caused McGerk some pain, and he stopped talking.

I asked Glick, "The publicity? Is that why you're willing to take the case pro bono? This story makes us sound like a couple of idiots, and like McGerk says, they didn't even get the facts right."

Glick put up his hand to interrupt. "I was on my way up to the U.P.—I come up here every winter to ski—when I read this *Free Press* piece at the Detroit airport. A really weird chain of events, your case. It interested me. I decided to put the skiing on hold for a day or two and check it out.

"But to answer your question, I'm not interested in publicity. Over the years I've represented hundreds—no, thousands—of people, most of them guilty as hell and many of them career criminals." Glick chuckled. "But I've never seen, or even heard of, a case where the perpetrators were repentant *before* they got caught. It's crazy, and certainly too good an opportunity for me to pass up. Representing you two would be like taking a vacation from working in the sewer. Besides, I want to make sure you guys get a fair shake."

He removed some papers from his case. "But before we get into the facts, perhaps you'd be kind enough to sign these representation forms—all of the pertinent information is typed in—so I can legally function as your attorney."

I looked at McGerk. He shrugged, not knowing what to say. No one we knew had the kind of money it would take to engage a good defense attorney.

"Give me a pen," I said.

We each signed the forms and Glick put them away. "Okay," he said. "Talk to me."

For the next thirty minutes, we told him everything. My involvement with Chris, the resulting huge credit-card bill, McGerk's robbery scheme, the snowmobiling lessons, waiting for the snowstorm, the robbery, and the events that followed.

"Chris also knows all the facts," I said. "From the hold-up note and surveillance tape on the TV news, she immediately knew that we were the robbers. She blew her stack and threatened to turn us in if we didn't do it ourselves. So, on Monday we tried to take the money back and make a run for it, but that didn't work. After we finally found out how much was really missing, we realized that the teller, Maria Grazzelli, had taken the lion's share. Chris helped us formulate the plan to get the forty thousand away from her. We pulled that off on Tuesday night when I lured Maria out to dinner and McGerk broke into her house and found the money. You know the rest."

Glick was astonished, hearing about Maria Grazzelli's involvement. "Are you kidding me? You only got twenty-six hundred and the teller ripped the bank off for forty thousand after you went out the door?"

"That's right," I said.

Glick shook his head in amazement. "You of course realize that no one knows that except you two, Chris, and Ms. Grazzelli. The authorities are convinced that you took all the money, and naturally this Grazzelli woman hasn't said a word to dispel that idea. She must be a hell of an actress. I heard that the police questioned her at some length about the gun, but she claimed it was intended for self-protection after being present at the other two robberies."

"I know why she had the gun," I said. "She was going to come after me to get the forty thousand back."

Another Glick head shake. "I've been practicing law for twenty-eight years, and this is the most bizarre case I've ever taken on."

"Will Chris get into trouble?" I needed to know.

Glick waved the question off. "From what I've heard, she's the only straight shooter in this game. Let's keep her involvement to ourselves." He looked at his watch. "Your guard mentioned that since you're both conscious, the police will probably be around this afternoon for booking and questioning. With the exception of your meetings with Chris, tell them exactly what you just told me. I'll be here with you in case it gets tricky."

McGerk couldn't believe it. "Ya want us t'confess to *everything*? I thought it wuz their job t'prove that we're guilty. Whut th'hell kind'a lawyer are ya?"

Glick ignored McGerk's insult. "There's too much evidence against you. Even being first-time offenders, make no mistake, you'll probably have to do some time for the robbery. What we're going to do is try to minimize the sentence."

"They'll never believe us when we tell them about Maria," I said. "It's her word against ours."

"Maybe that ain't quite true," McGerk said.

"What do you mean?" I asked.

McGerk rubbed his newly trimmed hair with his good hand. "We gotta ace in th'hole when it comes t'Maria."

Glick became interested. "Tell me about this ace in the hole."

❄

25

*A*t 3 P.M. law-enforcement personnel began filing into the small hospital room—an Ishpeming police detective, a Michigan State Police officer, one local FBI agent, a court reporter with a stenograph machine, and a police photographer. Abraham Glick, smiling but businesslike, handed out his cards to everyone.

The booking process began. Even though I'd seen it done on TV a thousand times, when the Ishpeming detective read us our rights it was like I'd never heard the words before. This was not television; this was the real thing and it was scary.

We were fingerprinted, and the photographer took mug shots. For the benefit of the record, the subject matter, date, time, location, names of the law-enforcement officers in attendance, and the names of the two suspects—Joseph Jarvi and Cornelius McGerk—were orally given to the clerk with the stenograph machine.

"Cornelius?" I exclaimed to McGerk. "Your real name is Cornelius?"

"Always hated that name," McGerk muttered from his bed.

The detective interrupted. "You will speak only when answering a question."

We settled down and the questioning began. With McGerk concurring, I did most of the talking. Following Glick's instructions, I told them everything except Chris's involvement. As expected, everyone registered total disbelief when I told them how Maria had embezzled forty thousand from the bank and about our retrieval of the money from her house.

"Maria Grazzelli?" exclaimed the Ishpeming detective. "Why, I've known Maria for twenty years! You tell a great story, but your imagination is really working overtime." He laughed at the absurd idea.

I glanced over at McGerk.

"You ever seen Maria's dog?" McGerk asked.

The detective nodded. "Sure. The big Doberman—mean sucker. She calls him Muffin." Everyone laughed.

McGerk continued. "Dog's wearin' a leather collar. You'll find a folded up fifty-dollar bill taped to th'inside of th'collar I put it there th'other night after I found th'money in the dog's bed—insurance against somethin' goin' wrong th'next mornin', which it did. The serial number on th'fifty is in sequence with those in one of the packets of fifties you guys recovered from us, that is if it wuzn't from the packet my partner let loose in th'wind."

"We recovered all of that money out on the highway," the state police officer stated.

"You guys could've planned all this in advance," the detective argued. "Taken a fifty-dollar bill out of your haul, broken into the Grazzelli house, disabled the dog, and put the fifty in his collar to corroborate your story."

Glick raised his hand in protest. "Really, gentlemen. Please keep in mind that there's ample proof that my clients are truly repentant. Remember, they tried to return the money to the bank. Do you sincerely believe that they'd undertake the task of concocting and executing such an elaborate scheme just to place the bulk of the blame on a teller, in the event they were caught?"

The detective got defensive. "Why not?"

Glick smiled sarcastically. "Don't forget that Ms. Grazzelli was the only person who had a weapon in the bank, and she used it. She attempted to kill my clients, using language that was only appropriate for someone who had been grievously wronged, the so-called wrong being the loss of forty thousand dollars that she embezzled from the bank. Inasmuch as you people have only just now become aware of Ms. Grazzelli's involvement in this matter, I assume that you haven't taken the opportunity to check the time tag on the surveillance-camera tape, documenting Mr. Jarvi's exit from the bank. Compare it against the actual time that the robbery was reported by the teller. If Ms. Grazzelli did indeed take forty thousand from the vault and then took it out to her car, there may be an unexplained gap of several minutes."

The detective, state police officer, and FBI man all looked at one another.

Our guard wasn't in the room when the sunlight filtering through the window awakened me the next morning.

"Where's the cop?" I asked the day nurse when she came in to check our temperatures and blood pressure.

"How should I know?" she replied coolly. "Nobody tells me anything around here."

When Chris came in I nearly wept with relief. She looked at my bandaged head with genuine concern, then smiled and gave me a careful but lingering kiss. The dark shadows under her eyes clearly indicated that she hadn't gotten much sleep. She went over and placed a sisterly kiss on McGerk's cheek.

"Good news, you're out on bail," Chris announced. "Your attorney apparently persuaded the judge to hold the arraignment hearing late yesterday afternoon, after you were questioned by the police. Glick requested that your presence be waived due to your injuries. The judge went along with it.

"Your attempt to return the money and the late-breaking development on Maria evidently were sufficient reasons to set a nominal bail. The trial is set for the fifteenth of March. Mr. Glick called me at home last night to explain it all. He should be on his way over here right now and we'll be taking you home."

"The bail money, where did it come from?"

"I put it up," Chris said.

"You did that for me?"

"Of course."

"Me too?" McGerk asked hopefully.

"You too," Chris replied. "I emptied my savings account. If you two skip town, I'll hunt you both down, break your crutches, and murder you with the jagged pieces."

I grasped Chris's hand tightly. "The cops, did they talk to you?"

She nodded and told us how on Wednesday afternoon the state police had arrived at her house and questioned her at length. Chris didn't have to feign shock on finding out about the capture, since she'd had classes at the university all morning and hadn't heard the news. She was more upset when they told her that we were in the Ishpeming hospital. She had tried unsuccessfully to see us on Wednesday, Thursday, and Friday.

"Whut's th'story with Maria?" McGerk asked.

Chris pulled up a chair. "According to the TV late news last night, Maria's been taken into custody. After they questioned you yesterday, the Ishpeming police obtained a search warrant and went to her house just as she was getting home from the bank. They made her take the collar off the dog. Guess what? Just as McGerk had said, there was a fifty-dollar bill taped to the inner side. Imagine Maria's surprise! The serial number on the fifty was in sequence with the others stolen from the bank. That, coupled with an unexplained time gap between Joe's exit from the bank and the time that Maria sounded the alarm, was enough to take her in on probable cause. The TV report didn't say what Maria told the police, but she's been booked. I guess the authorities are trying to sort this whole thing out now."

"Nothing to sort out," I grumbled. "We're all guilty, but Maria's a little more guilty than we are."

Chris smiled. "It's funny; that's what your attorney said on the late news. Somehow he'd arranged to get himself interviewed by a TV reporter after the police took Maria in.

"Everyone says that this is the juiciest news story to hit this area in quite awhile. They're all talking about the 'bank job.' People I don't even know are coming up to me, asking if you'd told me anything about the robbery beforehand and how well did I know Maria—stupid things like that."

"Jeezuz, is your job at the university in jeopardy?" I asked.

Chris shrugged. "I don't think so. They'd be letting themselves in for a lot of flak if they let me go just because I'm a friend of yours."

We could hear Glick's voice echoing through the hallway long before he came in, leading a reporter and video cameraman from the local television station. "You can shoot some footage of my clients if you like," he told them, "but they aren't making any statements at this time."

Neither of us had ever been the subject of any type of publicity. McGerk scowled uncertainly at the video camera while I did my best to put on an innocent face. The cameraman also wanted to get a shot of Chris, the femme fatale, but Glick objected strongly. He answered a few questions but smoothly deflected any details of the robbery and finally ushered the two of them out.

"Don't be surprised if you see a lot more media people before this is over," Glick said. "This story is getting more unbelievable by the minute, and the public is eating it up."

The doctor who had seen us the day before came in. He almost appeared relieved, saying, "Normally we'd keep you here a few more days for observation, but this isn't a normal situation. As soon as you made bail, the county no longer assumed responsibility for your medical expenses. In fact, that's probably why you were arraigned so quickly. So unless you're financially solvent—and being unsuccessful bank robbers, I'm assuming you're not—I have to release you immediately. But both of you should have a follow-up visit with your own doctor next week."

He examined us once more, and gave out prescriptions for pain medication. The big nurse bathed us, changed our dressings, and gave us instructions on keeping our injuries clean. We were taken to the front entrance in wheelchairs and released.

Chris and Glick carefully helped us into the attorney's large rented sports utility vehicle and transported us to my apartment. While Chris went grocery shopping, Glick ventured out and procured crutches, bandages, and our prescriptions. He even rented a hospital bed for McGerk which was promptly delivered and set up in my living room. Then Chris went over and paid the rent to my now-reluctant landlord, allowing McGerk and me to stay in the apartment for another month.

Since there was nothing more that Glick could do, he took off with his skis, promising to check in from time to time. His parting advice to all three of us was to keep a low profile—heads down and mouths shut.

Chris stayed with us through Sunday, preparing meals, changing our dressings, and generally making sure we could manage while she was at the university on Monday. She promised to return that night to cook dinner.

The Monday afternoon newspaper thumped against the front door. Although neither of us was in any shape to get up and retrieve it, we were anxious to read about Maria's arrest. McGerk, being the more mobile, limped over to the door on one crutch.

Although the police hadn't officially released details about how she'd become a suspect, the information had obviously been leaked to the press. The lead story on the front page covered Maria's arrest, describing how I had lured her out for a romantic dinner while McGerk searched her house and removed the stolen money after planting a fifty-dollar bill in the unconscious dog's collar. On a tip from McGerk, the Ishpeming police obtained a search warrant and found the fifty-dollar bill. The police arrested Maria on probable cause. The story concluded, saying that like McGerk and me, Maria had also engaged a lawyer who had obtained bail and her release from jail.

So all the bank robbers were now out walking the street, except of course, McGerk and I weren't doing much walking. The situation was depressing in the extreme. We were both physically incapacitated, financially destitute, and facing long jail terms.

McGerk painfully hobbled into the kitchen and grabbed a six-pack from the refrigerator. We were working on our first beer when the phone rang. McGerk picked it up.

He listened for a moment. "Oh, fer crissake!" He slammed down the receiver.

"What was that all about?" I asked.

McGerk fumed. "Sum idiot wantin' t'know if Maria Grazzelli an' I were lovers and wuz that why she shot me."

That was only the beginning. Everybody in the county must have read the story, because for the next two hours the phone didn't stop ringing. Someone from the flooring mill who barely knew me, a few of McGerk's customers from the garage, as well as complete strangers called to share their lengthy opinions on the entire matter. Through the front window I watched cars stopping at the apartment building, drivers gawking. Daring kids ran up to the window and yelled. Finally, we unplugged the phone, closed the blinds, and sat in the dark, drinking beer.

Sometime after 6 P.M. we heard a key slide into the lock.

McGerk smiled for the first time that day. "Thank gawd, Chris is here. I'm gettin' hungry an' we're runnin' outta beer."

Chris opened the door and entered, looking distraught, even frightened. She left the door open behind her.

"Hey, it's cold out there," I said. "Shut the do . . ."

Maria Grazzelli and her Doberman came in behind Chris.

"WHUT TH'HELL!" McGerk shouted, trying to get to his feet.

The Doberman lunged forward, snarling, fangs bared, stopping less than a foot from McGerk. Maria produced a revolver and pointed it at us.

The can of Bud slipped out of my hand and fell to the floor, spraying beer and foam across the carpeting.

26

"**S**he came up behind me with that gun when I got out of the car," Chris said in a subdued voice.

McGerk shrunk back into his chair as the Doberman continued snarling at close range.

"Don't give Muffin an excuse to tear your throat out," Maria advised McGerk. "He still remembers the other night when you fed him all that beer. He hated that hangover." Maria pointed to the wall near the front door. "Muffin, SIT!"

The dog obediently went over and sat down but continued to watch the three of us intently.

I tried to peer into the cylinder holes of the revolver to see if there were bullets in the gun, but the light was bad. Besides, the last time McGerk and I had seen Maria, she had been firing real bullets at us, so there wasn't any reason to think it wasn't loaded.

"What do you want?" I asked. I was scared. The only logical reason for Maria's visit was revenge, in which case I was the primary target.

She didn't answer me. Instead, she proceeded to unbutton her coat, carefully switching the gun from one hand to the other as she slid out of each sleeve. That done, she motioned at us with the revolver to go into the dining area. This was no easy task. McGerk and I struggled to get up out of our chairs and, using crutches and Chris's help, hobbled over to the dining-room table where we all sat down. At Maria's command, the Doberman came over and took up a position six feet away.

Maria looked at McGerk and me, decked out in our bandages, casts, and slings. "You two look like hell." Then, glaring at McGerk, she hissed, "You rotten bastard. All those times, years ago, when I invited you into my house and now you break in, steal my money, and get my dog drunk."

"Dog didn't seem t'mind it at all at th'time," McGerk said.

"Shut up!"

"Ya didn't haf'ta shoot me," McGerk added glumly.

"I wasn't trying to shoot you. I didn't even know you were there. With those helmets and masks, I couldn't tell who was who except when I saw all that money. Then I knew that Jarvi was one of the robbers." Maria swung the gun in my direction. "I was trying to shoot *him*!"

She fixed me with an evil eye. "You're the worst. Taking me out to a fancy restaurant, filling my head with romantic garbage while getting me drunk, then bringing me home and taking advantage of me while my guard dog is lying there helpless."

"Taking advantage of you?" Chris cried, then whipping her head toward me, "You swore that nothing happened!"

"Nothing *did*!" I countered loudly. "She was too drunk to remember anything. She fell asleep on the bed."

Maria used both of her thumbs to cock the hammer on the revolver. "Are you calling me a liar?"

No one said a word for several seconds.

"That ain't th'same gun you had in th'bank," McGerk observed. "This one's a .38." His comment released the mounting tension.

"The cops confiscated the .32 as evidence," Maria replied. "This one belonged to an old boyfriend of mine."

"Please uncock that hammer," I pleaded. "It's making me nervous."

Maria obliged and put the revolver into the pocket of her coat hanging on the back of the chair. "No need for guns; I don't have to tell you that if anyone tries anything, Muffin will tear him to pieces."

"I should have gotten the message when I saw the lipstick on the shirt," Chris muttered.

"NOTHING HAPPENED!" I yelled.

"Aren't you going to offer a girl a drink?" Maria asked no one in particular.

"Are you serious?" Chris blurted out, still angry.

"Of course I'm serious."

"What do you want to drink?"

"Ain't much beer left," McGerk said.

"No beer," Maria snapped. Then jerking her head toward me, adding, "Or none of that fancy wine that my 'boyfriend' likes. What else have you got?"

"We've got a bottle of brandy," I offered.

"That'll do. Make a pot of coffee. I feel like coffee and brandy tonight."

Chris got up, looked uncertainly at Muffin, and then went into the kitchen to fix the coffee. She brought the coffee and brandy over to the table, keeping a watchful eye on the dog. But the big Doberman, sensing that Chris wasn't a threat, just sat there and watched.

Maria poured generous dollops of brandy into the four cups. She passed them around, took a sip from hers, and fixed the three of us with a steady gaze.

She began talking. "I know you've already figured out a lot of this, but let me fill you in on all the facts.

"From the day I first reported for work at the bank I've been trying to figure out a way to get my hands on some of the money I was handling every day. But I needed a perfect plan—didn't want to take any chances on getting caught. I looked at the whole operation from every angle, but there were too many checks and balances. After several years I'd just about given up.

"Then you two yahoos decided to hold up the bank. When Joe handed me the holdup note, it was immediately obvious that this was an amateur operation. You two didn't even know that the armored car hadn't made it to the bank that morning because of the weather. I just played dumb about any money in the vault and let Joe take what I had in my cash drawer.

"As soon as he ran out the door, the idea hit me. The perfect plan! I hustled into the vault, grabbed forty thousand dollars and carried it out to the trunk of my car. Then I set off the alarm. I told the authorities that besides the cash in my drawer Joe had forced me to go into the vault and put packets of money into a bag that he'd given me. At the time, the cops bought the story without question."

I interrupted. "But all of that action would've been caught on the surveillance cameras. You didn't leave your window the whole time I was in the bank. I couldn't possibly have gotten that forty-thousand dollars from the vault. Didn't the cops look at the camera tapes?"

Maria smiled. "It's a rinky-dink system that only watches the front entrance. The camera doesn't view the tellers, the vault, or the back door. If Arne Laxso had put in a state-of-the-art surveillance system I could never have pulled off what I did."

She continued with her account. "So everything was cool. After the audit you two would be accused of robbing the bank of forty-two thousand dollars. In fact, I was praying that you wouldn't get caught. I didn't want you whining to the police that you'd only gotten two thousand and some change. They might've started asking more questions."

"How cum ya only took forty grand?" McGerk asked. "Wuz that

all there wuz in th'vault?"

Maria smiled again and shook her head. "We *always* keep a hundred thousand or more in the bank, but a hundred grand would've made a big bulge in the sacks you were carrying. The cops would've become suspicious when they reviewed the security-camera tape and saw the skinny sacks that you carried out. And I made it sound like I'd put one over on you, telling the authorities that I withheld most of the money in the vault. Both Laxso and the police said it was quick thinking on my part."

Gawd, I thought, the woman's got the mentality of a master criminal. Could this be the same person who collects stuffed bunnies?

Maria closed her eyes and slowly shook her head in frustration. She took a big gulp of the brandy-laced coffee and sighed. "But then you two decided to bring the money *back*. How could I have known you'd do something that stupid?"

She turned to me, "When you handed me the second note on Monday morning, I didn't know what to do. I tried to confuse you with that story about the new computer system, but I didn't think it'd work. Then Bruno LaFarge saved the day when he came up behind you at the window and made you panic, taking both the money and the note. My luck held out when the entire note wasn't legible on the security-camera tape. I thought I was home free. But I never thought you'd figure out my part in this whole thing and come after the forty grand. I didn't suspect a thing when Joe came to the bank and laid that big line on me in the vault, inviting me out to dinner. I just thought it was my lucky week."

Maria continued. "Then I got up the next morning, hung over, and couldn't understand what was wrong with poor Muffin. He was hung over. I only figured that out when I saw the beer in his water dish. Immediately I checked for the money, and it suddenly all fell into place. A setup. I was so pissed off that I put the .32 in my purse and took it to the bank, intending to go over to your place after work to get the money back. But when you two showed up at the bank and I saw one of you holding the whole forty-two thousand—forty of which was *mine*—and you were going to give it back to the bank, I just lost it and pulled out the gun."

Maria finished her coffee and handed the cup to Chris. "While you're getting me a refill, bring Muffin some water—he likes it in a casserole dish. It's going to be a long night."

"A long night?" Chris exclaimed. "Why is it going to be a long night?"

"We have to stay up and go over the details of tomorrow morning's job."

"Whut job?" McGerk asked.

"The bank robbery," Maria replied simply.

I almost dropped my coffee. "Bank robbery? What are you talking about? What bank?"

"Which bank have you had the most practice at?"

"Are you trying to say that you want us to help you rob the Hematite Bank tomorrow morning?"

"That's *exactly* what I'm saying."

From the kitchen, Chris leaned over the counter. "Are you crazy? You just got out on bail and now you're over here waving a gun in our faces and talking about robbing a bank—the same bank that these two already hit—and you expect them to help you?"

"They stole my money and now they're going to help me get some more, whether they like it not."

Chris gasped. "You're going to force Joe and McGerk to help you rob the bank?"

"It's too big a job for me. I need someone with experience in stealing vehicles and making getaways."

"Maria," I said in a reasonable tone, "you're up on an

embezzlement charge—a serious crime to be sure—but being a first-time offender you'll probably receive a lenient sentence—maybe five years, or even less. I realize that McGerk and I frustrated your plans for the forty thousand dollars and you want to strike back, but another robbery attempt on the same bank is absolutely insane. They've got to be on full alert now. Even if you get, say, a hundred thousand dollars, it wouldn't be worth the huge risk."

"How about *three million* dollars?" Maria said casually. "Would *that* be worth it?"

27

*M*cGerk half-smiled. "Three million—yer makin' that up, ain'cha?"

Maria leaned back in her chair, amused. "No, I'm not. You see, the problem with your robbery was that you didn't have an inside contact at the bank. You need to have advance knowledge of when money flows in and out of a bank."

I said, "Do you mean that there's three million dollars sitting in that bank right now?"

"Yes, but it'll be gone by midmorning tomorrow. That's why I'm here tonight."

"I don't believe it!" Chris exclaimed. "Why on earth would that little bank have so much money?"

"It's a new distribution system initiated by the Federal Reserve Bank in Minneapolis," Maria explained. "They send over one big currency delivery to one particular bank, and it's immediately dispersed to a network of local banks the following day. Saves money on transportation and labor costs. For security reasons, they'll be changing the recipient bank with each delivery, but the Hematite First National was the one they selected to receive the first delivery."

McGerk was skeptical. "Yer just a teller. How cum you know

that?"

"Arne Laxso naturally had the inside information but couldn't resist blabbing it to all of the tellers last week."

I said, "I'd think the Federal Reserve would have changed the initial delivery to a different bank after all of these so-called robberies at Hematite."

Maria shook her head. "Laxso wasn't going to let that happen—too much pride. When he first told us about our bank being selected, he was strutting around like a rooster in a barnyard, pleased as punch. After you guys pulled the job on Friday, he was worried about the Federal Reserve's reaction to it, but as soon as the cops captured you two last Wednesday, he immediately got on the phone to Minneapolis, letting them know that the robbers were in custody. Everything was fine up here, he said, and they could go ahead and send the big cash delivery.

"But unlike you morons, I checked to make sure that the delivery was made. This afternoon I sat in my car across from the bank until the armored car arrived. Judging by the number of trips the armored-car guards made into the bank, I'm sure they delivered the three million dollars on schedule. But all that money will promptly be shipped out at ten o'clock tomorrow morning to the local banks throughout the area."

Chris waved her hand at McGerk and me. "Look at these guys! You tell me how they could possibly rob a bank wearing those casts?"

"You're right; they'd be useless inside the bank. They'll be waiting outside in the vehicle that Mr. McGerk's going to steal. He'll also be the getaway driver." She turned to McGerk, "You've still got one good arm and one good leg, lover. Is that enough to manage another getaway from the bank?"

McGerk hesitated, looked helplessly at Chris and me, then nodded.

"You're going into the bank alone?" I asked Maria.

"No. Your girlfriend is coming in with me to haul the cash out while I keep everyone covered."

Chris stared open-mouthed at Maria. "ME? You expect *me* to help you rob the bank?"

Maria finished off her brandied coffee, her eyes taking on a hard, glassy glitter from the liquor. "What's the matter? Don't you think a couple of sweet young things like you and me can hold up one measly little bank?"

Chris shook her head vehemently. "You're absolutely crazy! I won't do it! No one knows that I was involved in any way with the *first* one."

Suddenly, the whole thing seemed so utterly ridiculous that I laughed at Maria. "Do you really think that you can force us to help you rob a bank? I don't think so."

Maria looked at her dog and pointed at me. "Muffin, HOLD!"

The big Doberman sprang from his sitting position near the dining-room wall and slammed into my chest with his huge front paws, knocking me to the floor. My head banged against a table leg, sending crushing waves of pain into my bandaged skull as I flailed around on my back. The dog stepped up onto my rib cage and thrust his muzzle within an inch of my nose, snarling and bathing my face with hot, foul breath.

"I just want to make sure everyone knows who's in control around here," Maria commented.

At the dining-room table Maria began sketching out the details for the morning's bank job. Chris, McGerk, and I sat in shocked silence, listening to her.

"We'll need one of those utility vehicles," Maria said, "big enough to carry the four of us, Muffin, and the bags of money. Before dawn, McGerk will find one and hot-wire it. At the bank, the guys will stay in the vehicle with Muffin, keeping the engine running. Joe's pretty useless, but we'll take him along just for the ride."

"I do holdup notes," I said defensively.

"Joe, shut up!" Chris snapped.

"I've already taken care of the note," Maria said, producing a plastic-wrapped piece of paper filled with pasted-on letters. "I worked in that bank for over ten years and I'm familiar with every operation. I know exactly what had to go into this note. They won't be able to get cute with me, and I won't have to say a word."

Chris interrupted her. "With that kind of money there, the bank is bound to be crawling with guards."

"They'll have one guard," Maria said, "and I know who he is—old Reino Niemi. We can thank Arne Laxso for that—cutting corners on manpower. Reino used to be a guard out at the mine, but he's retired now—only takes occasional part-time jobs. He's worked at the bank before. He'll have a gun, but he's fat and slow, and when I show him my revolver, he won't be a problem, believe me. I'll disarm him."

"Masks—what about masks?" Chris wailed. "You don't expect me to go in there with my bare face hanging out, do you? I'm a professor at the university!"

"Everything's out in my car, honey," Maria answered. "Ski masks, gloves, and bulky mackinaws to hide our shapes. They'll think the bank was held up by two short guys copycatting our master criminals here."

I poured straight brandy into my empty coffee cup and took a swallow to ease the pain. I felt terrible. My ribs and head hurt like hell from the attack by that damned dog. I hoped that nothing else had gotten broken.

"This is kidnapping—forcing us to go with you," I told Maria.

She shrugged. "In for a penny, in for a pound."

"After th'robbery, whut then?" McGerk asked.

Maria said, "We take off from the bank in the utility vehicle and go down a few of those side roads for several miles. Chris's car and mine will be parked somewhere along there—McGerk, you pick out a good spot since you know your way around. We'll leave the stolen vehicle there and Muffin and I will take off in my car. You three drive back to town in Chris's car and go over to Joe's apartment and pretend nothing happened."

I was astounded. "You're letting us go after the robbery? What makes you think we won't tell the police and the FBI exactly what happened?"

Maria grinned broadly. "Because you'd be giving up your share—a million dollars."

"Would you repeat that?" I said.

"Your share of the money—a million dollars. I'm a fair woman. I don't expect you to do this for nothing. We split the money up right on the spot; it'll only take a few seconds. The three of you get one million and I keep the rest."

"We don't want any of that money," Chris snapped.

McGerk and I looked at each other and then looked at Chris.

"You don't have any choice."

"What do you mean?" Chris asked.

"If you don't take your share, I'm dumping it right there on the road. You see, I want to spread the guilt around in case something goes wrong. I suggest you take the money. The police will probably be along that road any minute after the robbery."

"We'll tell them exactly what happened," Chris said.

Maria laughed. "That I kidnapped you, using my dog as a weapon, and forced you to rob the bank? Who'd believe that? It sounds too crazy. If you tell the police what happened, they'll immediately implicate you; after all, your credibility isn't the greatest. Bail will be revoked and you'll both wind up in jail. And do you really want to bring Chris into it? Remember, she's still clean. You'd do well to take the money and keep your mouths shut. With two of you just out of the hospital and still wearing those casts, you won't be suspects for this job. I suggest you think hard before telling people the truth."

After several moments of grim silence, McGerk asked, "Where are you goin' after we split?"

"The police think they're gonna send me up for embezzlement," Maria said bitterly, "but there's no way I'm gonna do time. Do you know what they do to women in prison? I'm going to jump bail and make a run for it—maybe over to Sault Ste Marie and into Canada. They won't be looking for a single woman and her dog."

"Ya won't make it," McGerk stated.

"I stand a good chance," Maria replied defensively.

McGerk shook his head. "Think about it. If we actually get th'three million bucks outta that bank—an' that's a very *big* if—it'll be the biggest robbery ever pulled off up here. Every cop in the U.P. will be on th'case. All three of us jus' got through robbin' that same bank, an' you better believe they'll cum lookin' fer all of us, don' make any difference that yer a woman or how busted up we are. We'd be prime suspects no matter what. An' when they find out yer gone, they'll put out an All Points Bulletin on you—fer jumpin' bail if nuthin' else. They'll nail ya long before ya ever get to the Soo. Hell, there's only so many roads up here, an' they'll have roadblocks up on every damned one of 'em."

McGerk paused, and then added, "Forget 'bout th'robbery, Maria. We won't say anything 'bout ya comin' here with that gun. We'll pretend the whole thing never happened." He slowly extended his good hand across the table. "Why don'cha gimme th'gun."

Chris and I exchanged glances. This was a new and strange McGerk speaking.

Maria stared down at McGerk's open hand on the table, not saying a word. A tear rolled down her cheek and she bit her lip. She reached over across the back of the chair and took out the revolver out of her coat pocket.

Then, gripping the revolver, she suddenly slammed the gun down on the tabletop with such force that I ducked, fully expecting it to go off. Startled, the Doberman leapt up and began barking and snarling at no one in particular.

Maria sobbed uncontrollably. "No! gawdammit, no! All my life I've wanted to be able to afford the nicer things—have enough money to buy expensive clothes, see London and Paris, eat in fine restaurants. Hell, I can't even read the *menus* in those places. With the forty thousand I had a chance to do some of that. Then you two Honest-Johns took my money, and now it's back in the bank. What idiots! Well, you're not going to sweet-talk me now. This is my last chance. If I don't make it this time, I'll be washing pots in some greasy-spoon restaurant for the rest of my life, that is if I ever get out of prison."

"I wuzn't tryin' to sweet-talk you," McGerk said carefully. "I really don't wanna see you get hurt or killed."

"Yeah, sure," Maria sniffed. "MUFFIN, SHUT UP AND SIT DOWN!" The big dog quit barking and sat down a short distance away, still grumbling and giving us dangerous looks.

McGerk leaned over toward her, talking in a soft voice. "Look, when we were goin' together I never told ya, but I wuz savin' up fer an' engagement ring before we had that fight and split up."

"You'll say just about anything to get this gun away from me, won't you?"

With difficulty, McGerk fished out his wallet, pulled out a slip of paper, and handed it to her. "This's the receipt fer th'last payment I made. It's been a lotta years, but they're still holdin' that ring fer me down at Main Street Jewelers."

Maria blinked at the receipt. "Why?"

"I dunno."

Maria began crying again. McGerk produced a handkerchief and she blew her nose loudly. "You're a sweet man, but you haven't been listening. What could we do on an auto mechanic's paycheck? We'd spend our lives clipping grocery coupons out of the Sunday paper, eating out at MacDonald's, and driving down to Green Bay whenever we could afford a big adventure. I want something better than that."

She continued, "Why don't you come with me? You handle yourself pretty well, and I don't want to get stuck alone in the snow with two million dollars in the trunk of the car. We'd still have plenty of money even after we give these two their share."

Chris and I looked at each other again. This was really getting weird.

"I don't want any a that money," McGerk replied. "I still luv ya, but we'd never be able to make it together with th'cops after us. An' they'd never give up lookin'."

"If you insist on pulling this robbery, keep it all," I said. "We won't say a thing."

Maria nodded with icy calm. "Okay, then I guess I'll make do with three million dollars."

The Doberman was still growling.

❄

28

*I*f you were to put stock in McGerk's philosophy about weather and bank robberies, then it was going to be a fine morning for a heist. A stiff north wind was already bringing in heavy amounts of lake-effect snow from Lake Superior.

McGerk was steering a stolen Jeep Cherokee around drifts already forming on the highway as we drove to the Hematite First National Bank. Before dawn, while the rest of us watched from Chris's car, McGerk, using one crutch, had hobbled over to a West Ishpeming driveway and hot-wired the brand-new vehicle.

I was sharing the passenger seat with Maria's dog, and neither the big Doberman nor I liked it. During the ride my left arm would brush against his huge shoulder from time to time and he would curl his upper lip and emit a serious growl. Sharp commands from Maria in the back seat were the only thing that held him in check.

I was in severe pain. My head pounded mercilessly, my rib cage throbbed, and to make matters worse, I had a terrible itch on my right leg beneath the cast.

McGerk pulled into the bank's parking lot which was curiously jammed with cars at nine in the morning.

"This ain't good," McGerk muttered. "Th'bank's fulla people."

Chris whispered hoarsely to Maria, seated next to her in the back seat. "Don't do it! There weren't any customers in the bank when the guys tried it. With a crowd of people in there, anything can happen. Somebody might get killed with you waving that gun around!"

"She's right," McGerk added earnestly, "It's too risky. Give it up."

"Too late to turn back now." Maria answered in a tight voice. She halfway pulled the revolver out of her coat pocket to show Chris. "Put on that ski mask, honey. We're going in."

Chris fumed nervously but put the mask on. The fierce weather, at least, lent some credibility to wearing it.

Maria leaned over the front seat. "Keep the engine running. I'm leaving Muffin right there between you. Don't even think about getting out. He'll tear off both your arms. Just sit tight and you'll be okay."

Maria put her ski mask on and pushed Chris out of the Cherokee ahead of her, then leaned back into the vehicle. "Muffin, STAY AND HOLD!"

The dog stiffened visibly. His muscles felt like rocks against my arm.

With her right hand jammed in the coat pocket holding the revolver, Maria grabbed Chris's elbow with the other hand and steered her toward the front door of the bank.

McGerk and I sat there like wooden Indians for several minutes, afraid to move a muscle, just staring through the windshield. I could feel the dog's body heat through the sleeve of my jacket.

A gunshot erupted from inside of the bank.

"Oh gawd! Oh gawd! She's shot the guard!" I moaned.

"Jeezuz, maybe the guard's shot *her*," McGerk blurted out.

Another shot.

"CHRIS! I'VE GOT TO GET TO CHRIS!" I yelled.

The dog didn't like all the commotion and let out a horrendous bark that reverberated inside of the Cherokee. He cocked his head toward me—teeth bared, snarling menacingly.

"Shut up, don't move, an' lissen t'me," McGerk said in a low, cautious voice. He slowly reached over to the ignition and turned the engine off. Then his hand crept over to the radio, turning the volume knob all the way up, and adjusting the speaker balance to full right speaker. That done, he carefully moved his fingers back to the ignition key.

"She gave him a Stay command, an' if I know anything 'bout dogs, he won't move offa that seat. I'm gonna try sumthin to distract him, and when I bail outta my door he'll probably lunge at me but'll stay put on th'seat. When he goes fer me, you get outta yer door like you had a rocket up yer ass. Got that?"

Out of the side of my mouth, I said, "He'll stay put, huh? McGerk, have you ever obedience-trained a dog?"

"No."

"Uh-huh." I turned my head slightly toward the Doberman. He had me fixed with both opaque brown eyes, his snarl steady, like an evil monster's snore. My right hand crept to the door handle. The cast on my leg felt like lead. I'd never make it.

McGerk flipped on the ignition and two hundred decibels of hard rock music jolted the Cherokee. The dog's head jerked toward the source of the violent sound coming from the right-hand speaker.

McGerk bashed the driver's door open with his shoulder and flew out in a tight ball. He almost lost his right arm as the Doberman whipped around and tore the sleeve of his mackinaw completely off.

I only caught a fleeting glimpse of McGerk's bailout because I was simultaneously slamming my body into the passenger-side door. My elbows had almost hit the snow-covered parking lot when there was a brutal snag on my rear end, followed by a loud ripping sound. Cold air rushed over my bare backside.

I scrambled to get up—forgetting that I had a cast on my right leg—and slipped around unceremoniously on my back in the snow.

I finally struggled to my feet. Both front doors on the Cherokee were hanging open, and the dog was standing on the middle of the seat, jerking his head from left to right, barking savagely at first McGerk, then me. But he didn't move off the front seat.

Wincing with pain from his leg wound, McGerk slammed the driver's door and limped as fast as he could around the front of the vehicle and kicked my door shut with his good leg. Trapped inside, the dog continued barking furiously.

I probed the seat of my pants, or what used to be the seat of my pants. I'd come within millimeters of losing my ass to the Doberman's fangs.

A third gunshot echoed from inside the bank.

Without crutches, McGerk and I hastily scrambled and slipped through the blowing snow over to the door and into the bank.

29

*T*he inside of the Hematite First National Bank had been transformed into a motion-picture set. Hi-tech filming equipment was everywhere. Large spotlights mounted on tall pole stands were casting harsh, white light on the walls. Fuzz-covered microphones on long booms and rolling cabinets of sound-test gear were being carefully positioned according to a large diagram of mysterious circles and squares that was easel-mounted in the center of the customer area. Thick, black cables connecting the numerous pieces of equipment snaked all over the floor.

Sun-bronzed men and women wearing headsets and holding professional video cameras, clipboards, or just cups of coffee were gathered in small groups. There was no banking business being conducted. The tellers were busy with lipstick, combs, and small makeup mirrors. Reino Niemi, the bank guard, had his cap off and was smoothing down his gray hair with one hand while unsuccessfully trying to suck in his large stomach.

Arne Laxso stood off to one side, smiling, rubbing his hands together, and trying hard to look reasonably intelligent. When he spotted McGerk and me leaning on each other for support at the front entrance, his smile dissolved into a cold, hard stare.

One man was holding a revolver, a thin wisp of smoke curling out of the barrel. He was huddled in lively conversation with a masculine-looking woman wearing a crewcut who kept pointing to a complicated meter in her hand.

Frantically, McGerk and I looked around for Maria and Chris. We finally spotted them through the crowd at the tellers' windows, next to a tall, bearded man dressed in a full-length fur coat. He had one arm firmly clasped around Maria's shoulders and was talking non-stop. However, she didn't seem to be listening, nor was Chris. They just stood there, dazed and helpless. The ski masks dangled from their hands.

The man in the fur coat looked up and saw McGerk and me and immediately interrupted his one-sided conversation. He strode over, smiling, hand extended.

"How about that! I can't believe my good fortune—first the embezzling teller strolls in and now the two bank robbers arrive in person! Where else but in a small town!" He energetically shook McGerk's hand and then grabbed mine so enthusiastically that, fighting for balance on my clumsy cast, I almost fell to the floor.

He kept grinning broadly, displaying a set of perfectly capped teeth. "I'm Derek Broadman, Associate Director for WorldCom Productions. You may not have heard of us, but we produce the WBC Network's new prime-time show on Tuesday nights—"Bizarre Crimes in America." Out-of-the-ordinary true crimes reenacted right at the scene.

"Last weekend we pulled your story off the AP wire, complete with photos. Incredible stuff! The bank job, embezzlement, then stealing the money from the embezzler while she's being wined and dined, attempting to bring the money back to the bank, the high-speed chase on snowmobiles—great!—made to order for our show! We jumped on a red-eye out of Burbank, picked up equipment from our affiliate station in Chicago, and drove up here yesterday."

McGerk and I began edging our way through the people and

equipment toward Chris and Maria. Broadman followed along and kept talking.

"We were just testing the acoustics for the final bank scene—perhaps you heard the gun shots—when these two young ladies happened to walk in. 'We're casting for more extras,' I told them. 'Take off those ski masks and let's have a look at you.' One of the hallmarks of our program is casting local people—adds a distinct aura of authenticity by capturing the regional accents, things like that. At first they didn't want to show their faces—Midwestern, small-town shyness I suppose. But I insisted. I couldn't believe it when one of them turns out to be Maria Grazzelli herself. And then you two show up." Broadman chuckled with glee. "Only in a small town!"

McGerk wasn't listening to Broadman. He limped up to Maria still standing at the teller's window, her hand jammed in her coat pocket with the revolver. McGerk slipped his hand into the pocket, covering hers, and began whispering in her ear.

Staring straight ahead, she nodded slightly as McGerk gently pulled her hand from the pocket, then slid his own back in and removed the gun, covertly slipping it into his mackinaw pocket. No one spotted the exchange. Maria, very pale now, didn't utter a word. Then her eyes filled with tears. She swayed against McGerk and laid her head on his chest and sobbed quietly. He put his arm protectively around her.

Derek Broadman was quick to notice this. "What do we have here?" firing the question at McGerk. "Only days ago this lady tries to kill you and now you're *friends*? Incredible! Tell me . . . tell me . . . I've got to know the latest twist."

McGerk smiled shyly. "Well, ya might say we're renewin' an old friendship."

"Gunplay sparks romance!" Broadman cried, writing furiously on a notepad. "Incredible!" He looked back at McGerk with interest. "Incidentally, that regional dialect of yours is charming!"

"Regional dialeck?" McGerk said, puzzled.

Dragging my snow-sodden cast across the floor, I moved over next to Chris. She was trembling, and I held her as tightly as I could while standing on one leg.

McGerk was beginning to get very nervous trying to exchange dialogue with Broadman. I stepped in to rescue him from the interrogation. "This is my friend, Chris Arquette," I explained to Broadman, nodding toward Chris standing next to me. "The four of us have been out on sort of a double date since last night, celebrating being out on bail, you know? The two girls came in to make a deposit an' left us waiting out in the vehicle. You know how these women are." I chuckled good-naturedly.

Chris settled down and picked up on our improvised scenario, "Gee, honey, those checks I was going to deposit—I must have left them at home. I guess we made the trip for nothing." Still shaken, she began pulling me toward the door.

Maria, also recovering now, joined the impromptu discussion. "Muffin, is he okay by himself out in the Cherokee?" she asked, dabbing her eyes.

McGerk grinned reassuringly, giving her shoulder a loving squeeze. "Muffin's jus' fine, sweetheart." He glanced briefly down at where his mackinaw sleeve should have been. "Such a sweet pooch he is, too. But I'm glad ya mentioned the Cherokee. We gotta get it back 'fore my friend out in West Ishpeming has t'use it this mornin'. He'll be pretty mad if he finds it's not there." He began pushing Maria toward the front entrance. "I think we better go now an' let these people finish their TV film."

But Broadman stopped us. "You're not going anywhere! I'm not going to let this fantastic opportunity slip through my fingers. The real criminals are always behind bars, and we have to use actors in our programs. But you three are here, out on bail. We'll use you in the filming, of course. The actual accused committing the reenactment—what publicity!"

"You want to film us robbing the bank?" I asked.

"Absolutely."

"An' it goes on TV?" McGerk asked.

"Nationwide—probably next month. The ratings will shoot through the roof when marketing gets the word out that the real perps are doing the show."

I corrected him, "*Alleged* perps."

"Alleged perps, of course," Broadman replied. "How could I be so tasteless. Well, what do you say?"

"Count me out," Maria said wearily, still clinging to McGerk. "I've had a rough couple of days."

"I don't wanna be on TV either," McGerk said.

"Besides, wouldn't it be illegal, us working for you?" I said, walking toward the door sideways to hide my bare butt from Broadman's view. "Isn't there a law prohibiting criminals from profiting from their crimes?"

"*Alleged* criminals—you just made that point yourself," Broadman countered. "And who said you'd make a profit?" He snapped his fingers at one of the guys standing nearby and crooked his finger. The man quickly came over.

"This is Larry Feldstein, one of our attorneys who irons out legal hassles when we're filming on site. Larry, can we work up an expense-only contract for these people?"

The man nodded. "No problem. I'll plug in my laptop and printer right now and have copies in a jiffy."

Of course, expenses can cover a lot of ground," Broadman said smoothly. He lightly tapped the bandage on my head. "We'll have to remove this dressing and your leg cast for several hours while you're on camera. Also, Mr. McGerk's cast. Replacing those will have to be done by your local medical people. Naturally, our production company will pick up your total hospital costs, probably until you're completely healed.

"And just this morning we saw a repair estimate for that fancy snowmobile that you two cracked up on the ice. Frightfully high. I imagine that place in Wisconsin will be after you to pay for it. However, it'll have to be as good as new for filming the chase scene some days from now—with you and Mr. McGerk on it for the closeup shots, of course. Repairing it will be another production expense covered by my organization." He looked at me slyly. "Get my drift?"

I nodded.

"Per diem expenses for all three of you, of course—might come in handy since you're not employed right now. I think we can extend the per diem for a month or so, up to about the time your trial date comes up."

We were all listening now.

"And finally, the most important aspect of all. I want to put a positive slant on this whole piece. Two young men in desperate financial straits, driven to the rash act of committing a bank robbery—but then repentant enough to go to dangerous lengths to make restitution. And the teller—a lifelong resident of the community succumbing to a terrible temptation placed in her path, making a single mistake that will haunt her for the rest of her life. I'm telling you, the viewing audience will eat up this episode! I wouldn't be surprised if the court of public opinion has a major impact on the verdict."

"Ya want me t'hot-wire a snowmobile on camera?" McGerk asked hopefully. "I kin hot-wire anything."

Arne Laxso came up, pointedly ignoring the rest of us, but flashing an ingratiating smile at Broadman. "I'm really sorry to interrupt, but I'll have to ask your people to move back for a few minutes. We have some bank business to conduct."

We all watched in silence as several armed guards transferred three million dollars to armored cars in the parking lot.

30

At the table next to us in the Landmark Inn's Sky Room, a young fellow having dinner with his lady friend recognized our party. Putting aside his filet mignon, he got up from his chair and came over, politely extending a small, pocket-sized notebook to me.

"May I have your autographs please?"

I smiled tolerantly and hastily scribbled on the open page. When this business of autographs started, weeks ago, I'd laboriously crafted legible signatures, prefixing them with warm little phrases like "Best Wishes To A Friend." Now I just scrawled my name—the way all celebrities do.

I passed the notebook on to Maria. She signed it and handed it to McGerk. McGerk wrote his name carefully, still not accustomed to having people ask for autographs.

There had been other changes in McGerk's life. Maria insisted that he had to shave every day and get his hair cut at least once a month. When Abraham Glick came up from Detroit for the trial, he took McGerk to downtown Marquette and bought him some new clothes. McGerk's old cronies at the Wild Goose Bar wouldn't have recognized him. But it didn't matter; he no longer patronized the place.

Other diners in the restaurant noticed us and began bringing over notebooks, business cards, and odd pieces of paper to be signed. Finally, Glick good naturedly had to tell them that we would take care of any and all autographs after our meal.

The waiter popped the cork on the 150-dollar-a-bottle French champagne and filled five crystal champagne glasses. Glick picked one up and held it high.

"Here's to crime," he proposed.

Chris frowning, lowered her glass. "I don't think I'm going to drink to that."

Glick laughed, "Well, how about, 'Here's to crime—it's not bad if you repent and are lucky enough to have Abraham Glick representing you.'"

Everyone laughed and touched glasses. I'd never liked champagne, but this evening was a special occasion that called for it.

The twentieth of March—the sentencing phase in the Michigan Circuit Court in downtown Marquette had concluded late this afternoon, and Glick had pulled off a legal triumph. McGerk and I had received suspended sentences.

I was still in shock. "Don't get me wrong," I said to Glick, "I'm not complaining, but how did we get off so easy? The jury found us guilty."

"The jury had no choice but to bring in a guilty verdict," Glick answered. "You did rob a bank—the evidence was indisputable. But it was also clear that, in all good faith, you did attempt to return the money—even the money that Maria embezzled.

"And Derek Broadman's TV show didn't hurt our case. Midwest morality triumphs over temptation, featuring comic relief funnier than any prime-time sitcom. With a message—if you screw up, it's never too late to make amends.

"So, all things considered, the court saw no good reason to put the two of you in jail. You'd repented before you were caught." Glick chuckled. "I personally think the judge was picturing the tons of hate mail he'd find in his in-basket if he came down too hard on you two. Hell, do you realize that you've become role models? And of course, we caught another lucky break when none of the people you stole snowmobiles from wanted to press charges. No harm, no foul, they claim. It seems they're just happy as clams that you two selected them to steal from. Now they can tell their friends about the famous bank robbers who stole their sleds to pull a job. Even Arctic Land isn't pressing charges. They're doing so much business now with people coming in to take a look at the Project X research sled in their showroom that they've completely written off the clothing gear that you wiped out in the accident. You guys certainly aren't short on luck."

Then Glick added, "But remember, this Circuit Court decision is a suspended sentence. There are rules to follow. If either of you screw up in any way, it'll mean real jail time, serving out the sentence without so much as a trial."

"Are we allowed to associate with each other?" I asked.

Glick smiled and nodded. "It took some in-chambers finagling with our good judge, but I convinced him that it was in the best interest of all concerned to allow you to consort." He waved his hand at McGerk and Maria who were sitting as close as they could get in two Chippendale chairs. "We didn't want any legal technicalities to break up this budding romance."

"What about me?" Maria asked hopefully. "Can you work any kind of deal at my trial?"

McGerk had urged Maria to drop her attorney and contact Glick about defending her on the embezzlement charge. Not only did Glick agree, but he offered Maria the same pro-bono deal that McGerk and I received. Maria's trial was coming up next week.

Glick took a sip of the expensive champagne but found it wasn't to his liking. He signaled the waiter and ordered a martini. "Your case is a bit different, Maria. However, you're a first-time offender, and taking the forty grand was an unpremeditated and impulsive act—at least that's what we're going to claim."

"Will I have to go to jail?" Maria asked.

"Probably, but I anticipate a light sentence. One thing in our favor—you'll have the same judge, and he's obviously in tune with public sentiment on this whole wacky case. Perhaps a year—two at the most—at a minimum security facility. Those places aren't bad at all."

"Two years?" Maria wailed. "And then I'll be an ex-con? I should have gone for the three million dollars!"

Glick quickly leaned across the table and stared hard at Maria. "Keep your voice down," he said forcibly. "Don't *ever* bring that up again—even among yourselves. You were damned fortunate that the WBC film crew was at the bank that day, or you would have done something irreversibly stupid and paid the price." He lowered his voice further. "No one besides us knows a thing about your 'three-million-dollar bank job,' so just forget it ever happened."

"I know *I'd* like t'ferget it," McGerk admitted. "Even th'dog'd like to forget it." He took Maria's hand and squeezed.

"Look at the up side," Chris told Maria. "You found McGerk and he'll be waiting for you."

"Damned right," McGerk exclaimed. "I'll be visitin' ya every week no matter what river they send ya up. Hell, I'll even take care of Muffin. I'm sort'a gettin' t'like that mutt."

Maria sniffed. "But where does an ex-embezzler find work when she comes back from up the river?"

"With me!" McGerk declared. "Got so much business at th'garage now that I don't know what to do with it all. I'm not kiddin'; ever since that TV program came out, people're bringin' in their cars fer any damned li'l thing just to sit around an' hear me talk 'bout th'robbery.

Guys askin' me so many questions about sleds that next winter I'm gonna have a line of used snowmobiles fer sale. Probab'y haft'a get a bigger place by then." He reached over and stroked the back of Maria's neck. Can't run it by myself anymore, I need a partner—somebody t'keep th'books. Whaddaya say?"

Maria took his hand off her neck and placed it on her cheek. "I say, quit doing that in public. Wait till we get home."

McGerk's eyes gleamed mischievously. "Kin we go over t'my place tonight? I'm tired of takin' all those damned stuffed rabbits off the bed."

Glick took a sip of his martini and smiled. "That's what I meant when I made the toast. Sometimes crime *does* pay."

"Well, it seems that everyone's life is getting sorted out except mine," I said. "All I'm doing these days is keeping house." I had given up the Ishpeming apartment and moved in with Chris. With the outcome of the trial uncertain, I hadn't tried to pick up a job but had gone back to work on the novel.

McGerk laughed. "I'll give ya a job, openin' my fan mail. Only pays minimum wage, though."

"But I've got prior experience," I countered sarcastically. "Every day I open plenty of my own—I just wish some of them were job offers. And the telephone calls. Even Uncle Paul called, inviting us all over for a meatball dinner any night we want to come. And after the trial this afternoon, I got out of the shower and there's this message on the answering machine to call some guy in New York City. New York City—how about that!"

Chris jerked her head toward me. "Who was it?"

"I don't know. I didn't call back."

"What's his name?"

"Hey, what is this—more interrogation? I don't remember his name."

"Did he, by any chance, mention the name Towbridge Hall?" Chris asked.

"That sounds familiar—I think that's it. Do you know this guy?"

Chris looked at her watch. "Six-thirty. Those people're usually at their desks until eight." She got up. "C'mon, we're going home, and you're going to return that call."

"Hey, I just ordered a medium-rare filet that Mr. Glick, our kind attorney, is paying for. What the hell's the rush?"

Chris jerked back my chair, saying to Glick, "Tell the chef to keep his steak warm. We'll be back."

The man kept talking and I kept nodding my head at the receiver as though he could see me. When I'd dialed the New York number, Chris had placed a pad of paper and pencil in front of me, knowing that it might be necessary to take notes. I was working on the third sheet when we finally hung up.

"My novel. The guy's an editor for Towbridge Hall—New York book publishers. They want to publish my novel when I finish it. I don't believe this—how could they possibly have known about my novel?"

Chris looked down to the carpet. "I was hoping you wouldn't mind, but I sent your manuscript in. I've known this Detroit literary agent for years. Normally, you can't get agents to even return your calls unless you're known. When the TV show aired, suddenly everyone knew you. That was the edge we needed."

Her eyes glistened with tears. "The novel is good, damned good, but without some kind of opening there was no hope that anyone at the big publishing houses would even look at it. But your name got the agent's attention and she agreed to read the manuscript. I made a copy and Fed Ex'd it to her. She called a week later and said that Towbridge Hall might be interested, especially since the author—namely you—is in the public eye."

"Why didn't you tell me?"

She shook her head. "I didn't know if anything would come of it, and you had enough problems. If they rejected it, you'd have felt even worse."

"He's arranging a round-trip ticket for me. I have to fly to New York right away to discuss some changes and sign a contract. He wanted to know if I could devote full time to finishing the manuscript. 'We have to move fast on it,' he said."

Chris came close and looked up at me. She gulped hard and wiped her cheeks with the back of her hand to stem the tears.

"He mentioned an advance," I added. "Didn't come out with an exact amount but said it would be enough to keep me going until I get an advance on my next book. Can you imagine that? He said my *next book*!"

Now Chris laughed and cried at the same time. "Maybe Glick was right. Maybe crime *does* pay sometimes."

I shook my head. "No, it doesn't. If it was just crime, McGerk and I would be sitting in jail right now." I kissed her and held her tight. "It was mainly you, and don't ever forget it."

On the way back to the Landmark Inn it had begun to snow, big fat flakes swirling down like the night in December when we were heading in the opposite direction.

As Chris had done on that night, I stuck my tongue out, trying to catch a few snowflakes.

"I'll tell you what we'll do after dinner," I said. "Follow McGerk and Maria back to Ishpeming, borrow the MACH 1, and take it out for an evening spin. Tomorrow's already the first day of spring, and you never know how many more good snowmobiling days will be left. I'm actually a pretty good sledder now."

Chris took my hand and leaned her head against my arm as we walked along. "Promise to go slow?"

"Uh-huh."

"No stopping at any banks along the way?"

"Aw, now you're taking all the fun out of it."

BIOGRAPHY

Jerry Harju was born in Ishpeming, Michigan, in 1933. He received a degree in engineering from the University of Michigan in 1957 and a M.S. from the University of Southern California in 1985. After thirty years as a manager in the aerospace industry in Southern California, Jerry began writing as a second career. His first three books, *Northern Reflections, Northern D'Lights,* and *Northern Passages* are collections of humorous short stories about his experiences growing up in Michigan's Upper Peninsula. His fourth book, *The Class of '57*, takes readers along a humorous and nostalgic path during Harju's six years of "higher education" at the University of Michigan. University life then—with its 1950's attitudes on world affairs, morality, and women's roles in society—was vastly different from today.

Harju now lives in Marquette, Michigan, spending his time writing books and newspaper columns and travelling all over the globe. His travels have included leading fly-in tours to Canada's high arctic, Greenland, and the North Pole.